Jillian's breath caught in her chest.

Michael Cutler was striding down the hallway. Tall, intent, his black hair rumpled. Wearing his uniform and needing a shave. Walking straight toward her.

She ran right up to him and locked her arms around his waist. "Are you all right? The news about the hostages—"

"Damn it, woman, I'm worried about *you*." He pressed his thumb against the swell of her bottom lip. "I don't scare easily, sweetheart, but your messages…"

"I'm okay. Better, now that you're here."

Instead of giving a verbal response, he took her by the shoulders and pushed her back against the wall. She quickly realized his pent-up desire had been intensified by fear and confusion and want. Because Jillian was feeling it, too.

JULIE MILLER

TAKEDOWN

HARLEQUIN®

TORONTO • NEW YORK • LONDON
AMSTERDAM • PARIS • SYDNEY • HAMBURG
STOCKHOLM • ATHENS • TOKYO • MILAN • MADRID
PRAGUE • WARSAW • BUDAPEST • AUCKLAND

For Norbert Wenzl. A true gentleman, a fun guy,
a kind soul. And my friend.

And for Cheryl Schuett. A smart, classy, talented lady.
Thank you for the immeasurable positive influence you
had on my son's life by teaching him to read music.

I'd work on a show with you two any day.
Thanks for reading my books and loving theater.

Recycling programs
for this product may
not exist in your area.

ISBN-13: 978-0-373-74522-7

TAKEDOWN

ABOUT THE AUTHOR

Julie Miller attributes her passion for writing romance to all those fairy tales she read growing up, and to shyness. Encouragement from her family to write down all those feelings she couldn't express became a love for the written word. She gets continued support from her fellow members of the Prairieland Romance Writers, where she serves as the resident "grammar goddess." This award-winning author and teacher has published several paranormal romances. Inspired by the likes of Agatha Christie and Encyclopedia Brown, Ms. Miller believes the only thing better than a good mystery is a good romance.

Born and raised in Missouri, she now lives in Nebraska with her husband, son and smiling guard dog, Maxie. Write to Julie at P.O. Box 5162, Grand Island, NE 68802-5162.

Books by Julie Miller

*The Precinct
**The Precinct: Vice Squad
†The Precinct: Brotherhood of the Badge

CAST OF CHARACTERS

Captain Michael Cutler—Commander of KCPD's premier SWAT team. A single father and seasoned warrior used to leading men, saving lives and guarding his heart. After burying his wife, he's not prepared to love again—especially a much younger woman.

Jillian Masterson—This physical therapist has fought hard to become a healthy adult—determined to make amends for the mistakes of her rebellious youth. Falling in love with the father of one of her patients isn't part of her life plan. Neither is her mysterious "admirer" who seems intent on ruining any chance at a successful life—permanently.

Mike Cutler, Jr.—The captain's teenage son has an attitude problem.

Troy Anthony—A patient of Jillian's.

Dylan Smith—A coworker at the hospital physical therapy clinic.

Dr. Wayne Randolph—He helped Jillian turn the corner in rehab.

Blake Rivers—Jillian's ex-boyfriend.

Isaac Rush—Drug dealer. A so-called friend from Jillian's former life.

Mr. Lynch—Rush family enforcer. You wouldn't want to meet him in a dark alley.

LaKeytah Anthony—An overworked, overworried grandmother.

Prologue

Jillian—

Your smile and your laugh light up a room even on the darkest of days. The rose I sent made you smile, I know. Perhaps white, the color of purity, would have been a more fitting choice, but I know that red is your favorite color. You look stunning in red.

Sometimes, I don't know which I love more—your kick-ass body or that sweet personality. You can be one of the guys or the sexiest woman in the room with equal ease, and that always keeps me guessing—and wanting more of you.

Jilly, I know, too, that there's something deeper inside you that most people don't notice. Pain. Vulnerability. Need. I notice. I've felt those same things, too.

I want you to know just how much I care

about you. I know where you've been—
what you've had to overcome—the difficult path that lies ahead. I understand that
we can show the world a strength we don't
necessarily feel inside. I admire that about
you—how you always keep fighting, even
when it's tough—maybe especially when
it's tough.

I just want you to know that you don't
have to keep fighting alone. I'm here for
you. If you need anything, you don't even
have to ask. I won't let anything—or anyone—hurt you ever again.

My heart will always be true to you.
I am forever,
Yours

While the letter printed off, he picked up the
snapshot of her unwrapping the ribbon and
plastic from around the flower he'd had deliv-
ered, and pressed a kiss to her adorably surprised expression. Then he dug a pin from the
desk drawer and gently tacked the photo on the
wall above the computer beside the collage of
similar images hanging there.

His favorite picture was one in faded black-
and-white newsprint, something from a state
high school basketball tournament. But he

knew Jilly's colors by heart. Long, dark brown hair. Eyes as bright and verdant as Celtic green.

And she was smiling. Right at him.

He smiled back and pulled the letter from the printer. Then, with clumsy gloved fingers, he pushed aside the gun and plastique, the ammo clips and clockwork devices, and cleared a spot on top of his desk to work. He folded the paper into three neat rectangles and stuffed it inside the matching envelope before rolling his chair away from the desk and heading out to deliver it.

Soon, she would know how much he had done for her, the risks he would take for her—all without complaint.

Soon, she would know how much he loved her.

Chapter One

"Nice shot, Troy!"

Jillian Masterson applauded as the basketball swished through the net.

Her young charge with the neat black braids pumped his fist in the air and whooped in victory. "Oh, yeah. I'm all that!"

"And a bag of chips," she cheered. He pushed his wheelchair beneath the basket to retrieve the ball while Jillian turned to her other patient and smiled. "Come on, Mike. Your turn."

"Basketball is lame," he groused.

Ignoring his ironic choice of words, she let his blue-eyed hatred for the world bounce off her skin and reached for his arms. Clamping one hand firmly around each wrist and bracing her feet in front of his, she pulled him out of his chair and balanced him against her shoulder while his leg braces locked into place. "Well, unless you want to plant some grass and turn this gym into an indoor football field, we're stuck with a basketball court. Let's try one from the free throw line."

"Why? It's not even a real court. Troy's baby brother could make a shot from that free throw line."

"You afraid you can't match up with an eighth grader?"

"I can do it," he argued. "I just don't want to."

"Show me."

"Jill…"

She stepped away, brushing the bangs from her eyes and shaking her ponytail down her back, forcing Mike Cutler, Jr.'s, reknit bones and weakened muscles to function on their own whether he liked it or not. She supposed the modified half-court in the university hospital's physical therapy center couldn't compete with the grass and fresh air and promise of the field where this high school athlete had once caught passes and run for touchdowns.

But she'd spare him the lucky-to-be-alive-get-over-yourself speech, knowing he wouldn't hear the words. She understood the black hole he was fighting to crawl out of. She'd lost her dreams when she was a teenager herself. Or rather, after her parents' tragic deaths in a plane crash, she'd single-handedly blown those dreams into smithereens, nearly ruining what was left of her older brother's and sister's lives as well as her own in the process.

Now, at twenty-eight, after rehab and long years of counseling and healing, she could look back objectively and see her mistakes, see that the love of her brother and sister, along with help and hope, had always been there for her. But Jillian would forever remember those dark days well enough to know that, at sixteen, Mike Cutler couldn't yet see beyond the fear, despair, anger and resentment that clouded his young life.

Instead of lecturing him, she stuck to the job she'd been trained to do—helping rebuild the bodies of accident victims and medical patients through physical therapy. And she was counting on the innate competitiveness of his sports-loving nature to help get the job done. Jillian reached down beside him to pick up the stainless steel cane from the polished wood floor beside him. Then she held out her arm and the cane, giving Mike the choice of which way he wanted to get himself to the free throw line eight feet away.

One of the advantages of standing five foot eleven herself was that she could look Young Mr. Attitude in the eye and not be intimidated by the width of his shoulders or the glare in his expression. "You gonna put your money where your mouth is and make the shot?"

"Do it, man." Troy Anthony put the ball in his lap and wheeled back over to their position. "If we don't play, then we'll have to go back to the weight room with the old farts and work out. I do *not* want to have Mrs. Hauser talking to me about her operation anymore. She smells like my great-grandmother used to. Creeps me out. And you know you don't want Old Man Wilkins talking to you about the Chiefs' off-season trades and recruitment again. That'd suck right down to your shorts."

Apparently willing to do anything to shut up his young compatriot, Mike snatched the cane from Jillian's hand. "Fine. I'll shoot the damn ball."

Jillian spared Troy a wink of thanks as Mike hobbled past her. She turned and studied the slight improvement in his jerky gait. A cataclysmic car crash had killed Mike's friend and shattered his legs. According to the medical reports Jillian had studied before writing up a therapy plan, it was a miracle that Mike Cutler was alive, much less walking. Several surgeries, steel pins and one determined father had gotten him to this point. But it would take a lot of patience—and convincing Mike to apply that stubborn attitude to his own recovery—to get him back to some semblance of normal life again.

"Here, bro." Once Mike had reached the free throw line and paused long enough to catch his breath, Troy shot him the ball.

Reading that split-second moment of terror in Mike's expression, Jillian reached around him and intercepted the straight-line pass. In one smooth movement that didn't allow either teen the time to feel embarrassment or regret, she tucked the ball against Mike's stomach, forcing him to steady it with his own hand. In the next second she took his cane, watching the muscles beneath his jeans and T-shirt clench and adjust to maintain his balance.

Good. Use what you've got, kid. You can do it.

Mike's athleticism would be as much a boon to his recovery as it had once been to her own. She'd remember to make good use of his natural balance and strength. Jillian bit down on the urge to cheer his success and pushed him a little further. "Dribble it."

An answering groan filled Mike's lungs with a deep, healthy breath. Jillian moved behind him, bracing his hips while he used different muscles and adjusted his equilibrium to control the bounce of the ball in front of him. She felt him tense his core muscles, stabilizing his body without any real help from her. *Excellent!* "Now shoot."

The normal bend of the knees to make such a shot couldn't yet happen, but the instincts were there. He raised the ball above his forehead, took sight of the net and pushed the ball off the tips of his long fingers. Jillian held her breath along with him as the ball arced through the air, hit the backboard and circled twice around the rim before dropping through the hoop.

"Yes!" She held up a hand and was rewarded with a high five. "Don't tell me basketball isn't your game."

Mike grinned. Stood a little taller. "Told you I could do it if I wanted to."

Uh-huh. Victory.

Troy rolled past him and the two teens touched fists. "Sweet, man."

Unexpected applause startled Jillian and drew their attention to the sidelines and the man standing in the doorway. "Nice shot, son."

Easy, girl. Flighty female had never been her style. She wasn't going to let her sick new pen pal turn her into a woman who jumped at the sound of a man's deep voice. Fixing a friendly smile on her face, Jillian calmed the startled leap of her pulse. "Captain Cutler."

Michael Cutler, Sr., filled the entrance to the

gym, his square, muscular frame cutting an impressive figure in his KCPD uniform—black from shoulder to toe, save for the white SWAT logo emblazoned on his chest pocket and ball cap, and the brass captain's bars and KCPD badge pin tacked to his collar. His sturdy bicep was marked by a black armband, his long legs by the gun strapped to his thigh.

Talk about sweet.

"Jillian." He touched two fingers to the brim of his cap and acknowledged her with a slight nod.

Though she guessed he had only a couple or three inches on her in height, and was probably fifteen years her senior, Jillian couldn't stop the quiet little flutter of breath that seemed to catch in her throat each time the widowed cop came by to pick up his son after a therapy session. There was something overtly masculine about the military clip of his salt-and-pepper hair and the laser beam intensity of his dark blue eyes. Or maybe it was just the mature confidence of a man at ease inside his own skin, evident in every stride as he pulled off his cap and crossed the gym floor, that made Jillian's neglected feminine hormones stand up and take notice.

Objective appreciation, she told herself. An attractive man was an attractive man at any age—especially one who kept himself in as good a shape as Michael Cutler.

"Ow."

His son, Mike, Jr., pinched Jillian's shoulder in a painful squeeze, jerking her from her wandering thoughts. "I need to sit down," he whispered between gritted teeth. "Now."

"Of course." Jillian hid the blush warming her cheeks by helping Mike walk toward the chair. It was less embarrassment than guilt at being distracted from her job that had her sliding her shoulder beneath his arm and anchoring her hands at his waist to guide him to his seat. Mike's balance might not be rock steady yet, but he was doing the bulk of the work, moving as quickly as his clumsy legs would let him. Maybe something had seized up with a cramp.

"Are you in pain?" his father asked, instantly standing behind the wheelchair like a wall of black granite to keep it still while Mike turned and plopped onto the seat.

"I'm fine, Dad," Mike insisted, shrugging off his father's hand while Jillian knelt down to adjust the foot rests and position his feet. She glanced up into the teen's downturned expression. Just as she suspected. The only thing cramping was Mike's attitude.

His father must have sensed it, too. With a measured sigh, he moved away from the chair and turned to greet Troy. He shook the young man's hand. "Staying out of trouble?"

"Yes, sir."

"How's your brother? Dex, isn't it?"

"Yeah. He made the honor roll last semester."

"Good for him. Good that he's got a big brother like you in his corner. And your grandmother?"

"Working. Two jobs. Like always. I might be getting a job pretty soon, too. As soon as I get this thing all figured out." He spun his chair in a tight circle, proving that, physically, at any rate, he was closer to healing than Michael's son. "I'm trying to finish my GED, too, but the math sucks."

Michael inclined his head toward his son. "Mike's pretty fair with numbers. He's in geometry at William Chrisman this year. Maybe he can coach you."

"Dad!"

Troy shrugged off Mike, Jr.'s, shut-up-and-don't-volunteer-me-for-anything reprimand, his own tone growing a little more subdued. "I'll get it figured out."

"I like hearing that. Good luck to you."

"Thanks."

Jillian stayed down longer than necessary so

that she wouldn't interrupt the man-to-man interchange that Troy got far too little of in his life. Even paralyzed below the waist and struggling to be the man in his family, Troy Anthony was still a big kid at heart. He beamed at the paternal approval in Captain Cutler's voice before wheeling over to Mike's side and thumping him on the arm. "Hey, will you be back on Monday, bro?"

Mike rolled his eyes, as if the Monday-Wednesday-Friday sessions he'd been attending for the last month and a half since mid-February would go on forever and ever. "I dunno."

"Jillian said if enough of us got together, we could play some hoops. She says there's a whole wheelchair league in Kansas City."

Go, Troy. Jillian had hoped that pairing up her two youngest charges in therapy sessions would boost their mental outlooks as well as their physical training. "With that upper body strength and the hands you've got," she observed, "you'd be a natural."

If anything, Mike grew even more sullen at her compliment. "I told you I hate basketball."

"Mike—" his father scolded.

But Troy was back in can't-touch-this form. He knew how to push Mike's buttons. "You hate losing, too?" He spun his chair toward the exit and took off. "Last one to the machine buys the pop."

A beat of silence passed before Jillian coyly prodded Mike. "Didn't you buy the sodas last time?"

"Hey!" With a sudden burst of movement, Mike raced after the other teen, his hands gliding along the wheels of his chair. "Get back here, loser."

"I ain't the one in last place, loser."

"Shouldn't you be walk—"

Jillian grabbed Michael, Sr.'s, arm, stopping him from going after the boys. His forearm muscles bunched beneath her fingers before he swung his attention back to her. "Shouldn't he be walking to build up his leg strength instead of getting more used to that damn chair?"

Jillian drew her hand away from the crisp sleeve and the solid man inside the uniform before her curious fingers dug into that warm flex of muscle. "Let him have a little fun. He's already put in a decent workout session today. Physically, he's reached a plateau and I don't want to burn him out."

Michael Cutler's eyes, as blue and dark as a twilight sky, assessed the shrug of her shoulders before zeroing in on her expression. "He'll continue to improve, won't he?"

"His doctors seem to think so." Jillian reminded him of the good news without sugar-coating the bad. "Mike needs to build his self-confidence as much as anything right now. He needs to care about moving on to the next stage of his recovery before more strength and coordination training will do him much good."

Michael, Sr., rubbed his palm over the top of his hair, making the black and silver spikes spring up in the wake of his hand. "Sorry. It always comes down to the mental game, doesn't it?"

Jillian nodded.

"I just get frustrated that he's missing out on so much. He's still only sixteen."

"Think about his frustration."

"He won't even talk to me about the night of the accident. I had to read the details in a police report."

"Does he share with his trauma counselor?" Jillian's own sessions with Dr. Randolph, the psychologist who'd helped her through rehab at the Boatman Clinic eleven years ago, and who remained a friend and occasional father confessor to this day, had been invaluable to her mental recovery as a teenager.

"Not much. You seem to be the only person he opens up to." Captain Cutler worked the brim of his cap with long, strong fingers before everything about him went utterly still—as if he'd suddenly realized his emotions were showing and he'd shut them down. Such precision, such control. No wonder other cops snapped to his commands. *Stop noticing details about the man, already.* Jillian focused on what he was saying, made sure she was listening as he slid the cap into his hip pocket and continued. "He doesn't have to play football anymore, or go to Harvard or get rich. I'd just like him to leave his room once in a while and walk without those damn braces—meet girls and hang out with his buddies and be a teenager again."

"Trust me, it'll happen." Jillian went to retrieve the basketball Troy had left on the floor. She knew that damaged people healed at different speeds, and that not even a father's unflinching support could force the process to go any faster. "He just needs time."

"Well, I'm glad you have the patience to deal with him. You had him smiling and trading high fives before he knew I was here. Seems everything I say or do ends up in a shouting match or him closing the door and not saying anything at all."

Jillian opened the storage bin outside the

equipment closet and dropped the ball in. "Just doing my job."

Michael Cutler was there to close the lid for her. His piercing eyes seemed to catch the light, even in the shadows from the stands and supports above them. "Working magic is more like it. He likes you. Likes coming here. It's just me at home since his mom passed away. Some nights, when he's shut up in his room and I can't figure out what he needs, it feels like he doesn't have anybody. I've thought about taking another leave of absence from work—like I did right after the accident—but then I think he prefers the time away from me."

"I'm sure that's not true."

"Don't count on it. I've negotiated with crazy people, talked kidnappers into releasing their hostages and convinced murderers to put down their guns. But I can't get my own son to open up to me. Pam—Mike's mother—she would have known how to talk to him, how to reach him."

A wistfulness briefly hushed his succinct tone at the mention of his late wife, making Jillian suspect that the father was missing the woman who'd been lost to cancer two years ago just as much as the son. Though she didn't know the details of Pam Cutler's death, Jillian knew the basics after discussions with Mike,

Jr.'s, doctor when they'd been planning his physical therapy. And she understood down to her bones how the loss of loved ones could wreak havoc on the family left behind.

The urge to reach out and offer a comforting touch was powerful. But Jillian reminded herself that they were little more than friendly acquaintances—that it was this man's son she cared about—and stuffed her wayward fingers into the pockets of her khaki slacks, instead.

"Don't be so hard on yourself, Captain." She called the cops she knew by rank or nickname, the same way her brother, an investigator for the district attorney's office, her sister the M.E., her sister-in-law the police commissioner and her KCPD brother-in-law did. "I know how hard it can be on family to see someone you love hurt like that. You want to help him—make things right. But you can't. The reality is, accident or not—Mike's still a teenager. He's going to have moods. And he's going to have to figure out for himself how to make this work. In the end, the best thing you can do for him is love him."

Those blue eyes narrowed, silently asking a question. Yes, she was speaking from personal experience, but Mike's dad didn't need to know everything about her sordid past.

When she turned away to get her clipboard and wristband of keys, he followed her, letting her pretend she had no shameful secrets to keep. "He's got that. The love, I mean."

"Mike knows that, down inside. He may not remember it every day, but he knows you love him. Just the fact that you use your dinner break to bring him here to the clinic and pick him up means something to him." Jillian slipped the elastic key bracelet around her wrist and tucked the clipboard of treatment logs under her arm. Together, they headed toward the gym exit and the hallway beyond. "Look at Troy, on the other hand. He's fighting most of his recovery battle on his own. Ever since the shooting, his grandmother refuses to leave his brother, Dexter, alone. Either he's at school or she locks Troy in the apartment with him to keep an eye on him the evenings she works her second job."

"It can't be easy for her."

"I'm sure it's not—and I admire her for supporting her grandkids financially, but it's almost as if she's given up on saving Troy and is focusing all her energy on Dexter. If Troy wants to come to physical therapy he has to schedule the appointments himself and take the bus to get here. I've been giving him a ride home, at least, trying to give him a little extra attention and ease some of the burden."

"You're driving him home tonight?" The captain stopped, checked his watch. It wasn't five o'clock yet, and she'd done it more than a dozen times. No big deal.

She turned at the doorway arch. "As soon as I log in these stats and sign out."

"Where does he live?"

Jillian named the street and apartment area just west of downtown Kansas City. His mouth thinned as he propped his hands on his hips. "At HQ we call that neighborhood No-Man's Land. It's not the safest place to be after dark."

"Clearly. Otherwise, Troy might not have been shot in the back by that stray bullet."

"I'm serious, Jillian."

Did he see her laughing? She knew about the dangers of No-Man's Land—more personally than Michael Cutler would probably imagine. If she could keep Troy from falling prey to them the way she once had by simply giving the kid a little extra time and offering him a ride, she would. "I don't take chances I don't have to. But I'm not going to let Troy shoulder his recovery all by himself, either. Somebody always knows when I leave and where I'm going."

"And when you get back?"

Jillian groaned. "It's just a car ride. I can handle it, Captain."

His low-pitched curse followed her into the hallway as she locked the gym door behind them. "I'm not your commanding officer, so why don't you call me Michael? That'd be a damn sight friendlier than 'ugh' or 'whatever,' which seems to be all I'm hearing from Mike these days."

Jillian relaxed enough to smile, glad his disapproval of her efforts to help Troy had been short-lived. "Captain Ugh. I bet your men would love to call you that."

"My men wouldn't dare. Not to my face." Instead of heading past her door to get Mike from the break room, he followed her into her office. "Can you spare another minute?"

"Sure." Jillian hugged the clipboard to her chest and turned.

"I wanted to double-check the PT schedule. Mike's school is having their spring break next week. He's pretty bummed about making up extra class work while his classmates go on vacation, and since he seems to enjoy his time with you and Troy, I wanted to see if I could still bring him in for his regular sessions—give him a break from history and geometry and…me."

"I'll be here," Jillian promised. "Anything else I can do to help?"

"Yeah. Be careful driving through No-Man's Land. My son needs you." He pulled his SWAT cap from his back pocket and pulled it on over his head. The stern police captain had returned. "Keep your doors locked. If you feel threatened in any way, stay in your car and drive straight to the nearest police station. Run red lights if you have to. If you think someone is following you, stay in your car and honk the horn until an officer comes out to assist you."

"You know, I have a big brother to give me lectures like that. You don't have to."

"As long as you listen to one of us. I can give Troy a lift home on the days I'm off duty and don't have to get back to the precinct." He adjusted the brim of his cap to shade his eyes. "If riding with a cop wouldn't cramp his style."

"That's nice to offer. I'll ask him."

"Be careful. Mike's counting on you."

Look who was talking. She dropped her gaze to the sidearm holstered at his thigh. "You be careful."

"Always."

After he tipped his hat and left, Jillian watched him stride down the hallway. Yeah. Big-brotherly overprotection aside, fortysomething looked good on the police captain from this view, too.

Savoring the responding skitter of her pulse, Jillian turned to her desk. Her gaze landed on the droopy, fading flower in the glass vase there, and her heart rate kicked up another notch. Would it have killed the sender to include a note? Or even just a name?

Between friendly discussion and heated debates, she'd forgotten for a few minutes that not all men were as straightforward as Michael Cutler. Maybe she was only crushing on the older man because she was 99.9 percent certain he hadn't sent her that mysterious rose. As beautiful and blameless as the deep red flower might once have been, she'd lived with too many deceptions in her life already. The whole secret admirer thing had lost its charm long ago.

Dismissing the tiresome joke with a shake of her head, Jillian sat behind her desk, pulling up Mike's and Troy's files on her computer to chart the updates. But the rose kept taunting her from the corner of her eye.

It was the sort of apologetic gesture her ex-boyfriend, Blake Rivers, would have made to get himself out of trouble with her. She supposed breaking up with him after an attempt to rekindle a relationship—clean and sober style—had failed qualified as trouble. But she had no proof the flower had come from Blake. No reason to suspect him. She'd left him months ago. He'd moved on to some blond reporter or red-haired heiress, according to the paper's society page. Jillian was old news.

And she intended to stay that way. As wealthy and handsome and devilishly clever as Blake might be, he had a reckless streak in him that had enabled her own addiction and nearly gotten them both killed. Jillian had promised her family, her therapist Dr. Randolph and herself that she was never going to go down that dangerous, self-destructive path again.

But if not Blake, then who had sent her the flower?

She supposed a phone call to Blake's office at Caldwell Technologies couldn't hurt. She didn't want to send any false signals to her ex, but a few words to put her mind at ease and set him straight on the romance-is-over message was worth the risk. And if the rose wasn't from Blake…?

Jillian was leaving a message on Blake's answering machine, reluctantly asking him to return her call, when Dylan Smith, another physical therapist who worked at the hospital's outpatient therapy clinic with her, knocked on her door. She waved him into the room as she hung up the phone. As usual, Dylan's dimpled cheeks and mischievous grin demanded she smile in return.

"What's cookin', Masterson?" He shoved his fingers through his muss of blond hair and sat down. "Makin' plans for a hot date?"

"I'm workin', Smith. Aren't you?"

"Hell, no. It's five o'clock, it's Friday and a bunch of us are going over to the Shamrock to hit happy hour. If you don't have plans, come with us."

The Shamrock Bar? Fun with her friends sounded tempting, but her drinking days were over. "Thanks for the invite, but I've got things to do at home this weekend."

"I helped you move into that apartment—up three flights of stairs, I might add—and everything looked neat and pretty and sitting in its place before we all left. Come."

Jillian grinned at his pitiful, boyish pout. "My bedroom is only half painted, and the dueling colors have been driving me nuts all week. We're supposed to have rain this weekend, and if I can't open the windows and work, I'll have to suffer through Pepto-Bismol pink and ice blue for another whole week. I need to get started on it tonight."

Dylan leaned forward, reached across the desk and laid his hand over the top of hers where it rested on the blotter. Every muscle in Jillian's fingers froze at the unexpected touch, though she managed to keep her smile in place.

"Just for an hour or two, Jilly? Please?" Dylan coaxed.

"I can't."

"I've got a bet with that new occupational therapist that I can eat an entire serving of the Shamrock's fried habaneros and win free drinks for a year. You can cheer me on."

"Or bring the stomach pump you'll need when you're done."

"Very funny. Where's the love?"

There was nothing secret about Dylan's harmless flirtations. If you were female, he flirted. Still, boyish charm aside, Jillian thought it wise to steer clear of romantic entanglements for now, and gently extricated her hand from his. "Sorry. Ask the O.T. to cheer you on. She's a hottie and it sounds like she might be interested in you. Share your habanero breath with her."

"You've got to have fun sometime." Dylan pushed to his feet, his grin firmly locked into place. He placed his hand over his heart and made a slight bow. "And I'm your man whenever you're ready. Oh, I forgot."

He reached inside the royal-blue polo shirt that matched her own clinic uniform, pulled out an envelope and set it on her desk.

"What's this?"

"Lulu at the front desk was on her way out. She asked me to deliver it to you."

Please, no. Jillian gingerly picked it up. No return address, and though the envelope had a stamp, it hadn't been canceled. But the name and clinic address clearly belonged to her. An uneasy feeling soured her lips into a frown. "I thought the mail already came."

Dylan plunged his hands into his pockets. "It must have dropped behind the counter or something."

Jillian shrugged off the perplexing mystery and slid her finger beneath the flap to open it. "Thanks."

He nodded toward the corner of her desk. "By the way, your flower needs some water."

"Don't you think it's a little late for that?" Enough with the torment. Jillian plucked the dead rose from the vase and dropped it into the trash. "I should have sent it over to the main hospital for a patient who'd take better care of it than I did. My bad."

His gaze seemed to fix on the fallen flower for a moment before the grin returned. "Not a green thumb, huh? I'll make a point to remember that next Valentine's Day."

"Bye, Dylan. Don't forget to take a gallon of milk and a fire extinguisher with you. Good luck, you idiot."

The blond charmer left with a laugh. Once she was alone, Jillian took a deep breath, pulled out the letter and leaned back in her chair to read it.

She slapped her hand over her mouth to keep from crying out.

MICHAEL HAD SEEN THAT LOOK on the faces of parents waiting outside a school building locked down because of an armed intruder or bomb threat. He'd seen that look on a hostage-taker who'd gone off his meds and didn't understand why he'd been shot by one of Michael's SWAT team.

He hadn't expected to see it on Jillian Masterson's youthful face when he raised his hand to knock on her open office door.

Shock. Helplessness. Fear.

"Are you all right?"

Green eyes darted up to his and she jumped to her feet, sending her chair crashing back into the wall behind her desk. By the time she'd groused and righted the chair and spun around to face him, her cheeks were flushed a rosy color. He'd clearly startled her. Again.

"What…are you doing here?" she stammered.

His negotiator's instincts kept his voice calm, his movements slow and precise as he stepped into the room. Whatever was wrong here, he didn't want to aggravate the problem. "I forgot Mike's cane. The gym's locked. Are you all right?" he repeated.

Jillian wadded up the letter that was already half crushed in her fist and shot it into the trash can beside her desk. "I'm fine."

And he was the tooth fairy. "Was that bad news?"

She swept aside a strand of coffee-colored hair that had fallen across her cheek and tucked it into the long, sleek ponytail at her nape. Then she was circling her desk, pulling the keys off her wrist, offering him a smile he didn't believe. "It's just one of those chain letters. You know, send it on to so many people and you'll get a bunch of stuff in return. Annoying, aren't they?"

He wouldn't know. But he did recognize a load of BS when he heard it. "Jillian—"

"I need to sign out ASAP so I can get Troy home before dark. I'll be right back so you don't have to keep Mike waiting."

Miles of long legs and the graceful athleticism of her walk quickly carried her down the hallway and around the corner. *Conversation over, old man. Take the hint.*

For a moment, Michael debated between trusting his instincts about people and minding his own business. But he'd spent too many years as a cop, training his mind and body to pay attention to the warning signs people gave him, to let her behavior go without an explanation. It was always easier to stop trouble before it got started.

Pretty, sassy, make-his-son-smile Jillian Masterson was in trouble.

Making sure he was alone in her office, he plucked the paper wad she'd tossed out of the trash can and unfolded it, smoothing it open against his thigh. He read it quickly. Read it again. Frowned.

A love letter.

One that made a healthy woman go pale, jump at his approach and toss the missive away with a flippant excuse before bolting from the room.

Right. Nothing suspicious about that.

Chapter Two

"Can you get it, Troy?"

"Yeah, I'm good."

Jillian closed the passenger-side door of her dark blue SUV, pressed the automatic locks and turned a slow 360 to take note of the traffic, parked cars and local residents up and down both sides of the drab, run-down city block. There were patches of brightness and warmth here and there where hope and promise tried to shine through. A freshly painted window box waited for spring flowers to be planted. A trio of preteen girls sat on the stoop across the street, chattering in laughing voices under the rosy glow of the setting sun. Construction signs promised a condemned building was about to be razed and replaced by something clean and new.

But she was just as aware of the weary posture of the shopkeepers locking their doors and pulling down protective cages, the curious glances and quick dismissals from workers climbing off the bus at the corner and hurrying toward their respective homes before any kind of trouble found them. And she couldn't miss the homeless man, dragging a filthy backpack behind him as he turned into an alley and disappeared.

Thankfully, though, there were no pimps, no gangbangers, no visible dealers she recognized from those lost days a decade ago when the dark corners and hidden secrets of this Kansas City neighborhood had offered her a false escape from the sorrows and stress of her teenage life. Of course, night hadn't fallen yet. Shadows and moonlight were usually the only invitation the cockroaches needed to come out of their holes.

A shiver of remembered nightmares rippled across her skin, leaving a sea of goose bumps in its wake.

You've moved beyond this place, she reminded herself with a mental nod, shaking off the sudden chill. She was older, wiser and ten years clean without a fix of coke. To her dying day, she'd atone for that wasted part of her life by helping youths like Troy Anthony move beyond the sucking trap of No-Man's Land the way she finally had. *So do it, already.*

"Wait up." Zipping the front of her sweatshirt jacket, Jillian hurried to catch up to Troy as he maneuvered his chair over the curb onto the sidewalk. She grabbed the handles and steered him up the concrete ramp that zigzagged beside the stairs leading to the apartment building's double doors. "I promised front door service, and that means apartment 517."

Troy turned his key in the lock of the inner lobby door. "Ain't nothing wrong with these magic hands. I can get up to the fifth floor by myself. You'd better head on home before dark."

"Is everybody my big brother today? This'll take like, what, five minutes max?" Jillian rolled him across the cracked tiles of the lobby floor, and waited while he pushed the elevator's call button. The numbers over the elevator doors didn't light up, but she could tell from the grinding of gears and cables that the car was descending inside the shaft. "I don't want your grandmother to worry about you getting home safely. She's got enough on her plate."

"You're sure you're not coming upstairs to snitch one of her chocolate chip cookies?"

"Hey, if somebody offers me homemade cookies and there's chocolate involved…" Jillian waved her arms out in a dramatic gesture. "Ahh!"

Their shared laughter ended abruptly when the light beside the super's door clicked on. Jillian clutched her fists back to her chest and she masked the catch in her throat with a cough. Great. Since when had she gotten so skittish?

Stupid letter. Stupid flower.

She smoothed her hair into her ponytail and tried to ease her paranoia by taking stock of her surroundings inside the lobby. She and Troy were alone. The super's light must be rigged with some kind of motion sensor that she had inadvertently set off, because no one else had entered the building behind them or come out of the apartment. She should be relieved the light had snapped on because it dispelled the evening gloom gathering in the lobby, although the corridor beyond the super's apartment remained in shadows. She *was* relieved. For a moment. Deliberately focusing her senses also gave her a whiff of a pungent odor that was decidedly less pleasant than the aroma of freshly baked cookies she imagined coming from Troy's apartment.

Jillian wrinkled up her nose. "What is that smell?"

"Probably Mrs. Chambers's cats in 102. She can't say no to a stray. You all right?"

"Yeah, I'm fine. I think somebody needs to change the litter box."

"You sure? You seem a little rattled."

"Just tired. It's been a long day." A final ding of the elevator gave her the perfect excuse to brush aside Troy's concerns. As the steel doors parted, she grabbed the handles on Troy's wheelchair. "The Jillian Masterson chauffeur service is ready to—"

"There you are. Where have you been? You're late. Way late." A sharp voice from inside the elevator greeted them before the tall, stout black woman braced the doors open with her thick, gnarled fingers.

"Grandma—"

"Don't you *Grandma* me."

Jillian pulled the chair back as LaKeytah Anthony stormed out. The older woman with the purplish-dyed hair reached out to her grandson to give him a tweak on his chin and a light cuff on his ear in one smooth motion. "Dex is upstairs by himself, doin' his homework. You were supposed to have him here forty minutes ago. Now I'll be late gettin' to my shift at the Winthrop Building."

"I'm sorry, Mrs. Anthony. I got held up at the office for a few minutes. Troy called."

"An hour ago!"

"It's rush hour," Troy defended. "Jillian drove as quick as she could. You know there's construction and stuff."

LaKeytah wouldn't hear it. "I thought the whole idea of you drivin' him was to get him home early. You know what I'm fearin' when I don't know where my boys are."

The *idea* was to get Troy to therapy, period. Saving the Anthonys time, money and concern was supposed to be the bonus. "It wasn't my intent to worry you."

"I can't get to work if he isn't here."

"Dex is fourteen," Troy argued. "He can be by himself for half an hour."

"How old were you when you got shot?"

"Mrs. Anthony!"

The older woman's fatigue was evident as she finally paused to catch her breath. "Maybe if I'd been here to walk you home that night…"

"Then maybe you'd have got shot, too."

Dismissing the sad logic of Troy's words, LaKeytah straightened and pointed a stern finger at him. "Dinner's in the microwave. Make sure Dex finishes his algebra." The accusatory finger swung toward Jillian. "I'm gonna be late to clean my offices now, thanks to you. If you want to help Troy, you get him home on time." With a grunt and a glare, LaKeytah stormed outside, letting the lobby's double doors slam shut behind her.

A beat of shocked silence passed before Troy

leaned forward to open the elevator doors again. "Sorry about that."

Still feeling a sting of guilt, Jillian summoned a wry smile. LaKeytah Anthony worked two jobs, raised two teenagers and had plenty of reason to worry about her family in this neighborhood. Though she didn't appreciate being anyone's whipping post, Jillian thought she could understand the other woman's anger. "Your grandmother's stressed out about work, and like she said, she's concerned about you."

"She's concerned about Dexter." He rolled his eyes to punctuate his mocking acceptance that *he* was the grandson LaKeytah had already given up on. "She just wants me home so I can babysit."

"Troy." Jillian squeezed his shoulder. "It's more than that."

He shrugged off her offer of comfort. "She's got no cause to jump your case like that."

"Forget it." She wheeled him inside and let him position his chair while she pushed button number 5.

"I can get upstairs on my own."

"I know you can. But I promised to see you home, okay? Home's the fifth floor." The doors drifted shut. Let him be all tough and hide the hurt he must be feeling—Jillian was still going to care. "Besides, if anything

happens to you between here and there, I
don't want your grandmother chewing me
another new one."

"I hear that." Troy grinned.

Jillian relaxed. He was going to be okay.

HE SILENTLY PULLED THE DOOR SHUT behind him
and crept out of the shadowed hallway into the
lobby, his senses finely tuned to the sweet scent
of Jillian Masterson, despite the ammonia odor
of soured kitty litter that left his eyes watering.

A terrible sense of right and wrong burned
through his belly. What he'd just overheard had
been wrong. All wrong.

He needed to make it right.

The old woman in apartment 102 had gener-
ously opened her door to give him directions to
Troy Anthony's place. It had probably been
more foolish than generous for the old cat freak
to unlock her door to a stranger—but not as
foolish as the woman who'd just reamed Jillian
up one side and down the other for no good
reason. Grandma Anthony's harsh words had
upset Jillian, he could tell. She was worried
about the boy, too.

She smiled and tried to apologize, even joked
with the kid afterward, but he could tell.

Nobody upset his sweet Jillian.

And got away with it.

JILLIAN SWALLOWED THE LAST BITE of the rich chocolate chip cookie and laughed as the two Anthony brothers dutifully closed the cookie jar and reached for their dinner plates to cut up their chicken. Dessert first had lightened Troy's mood, the sun was setting and it was time for Jillian to say her goodbyes and go home.

She plucked a stray cookie crumb from the sleeve of her jacket and popped it into her mouth before pushing her chair away from the kitchen table. "Don't forget to study for your GED, Troy." She winked at his younger brother. "You'll have to have Dex help you with the math."

Dexter laughed. "I will if you teach me how to dunk."

Troy rolled his eyes and put his big hand over Dexter's face, pushing the grin aside in a timeless gesture of brotherly annoyance.

Good. LaKeytah's lecture, the resulting guilt and the challenges of coping with his disability had all receded to manageable levels for Troy, and his attitude seemed fixed firmly back in the positive position. Jillian had trouble masking her own smile at his resiliency. Everything in Troy's apartment seemed clean, relatively clear of obstacles to his wheelchair and safe. He would be okay. "Call me if you need something. Otherwise, I'll see you Monday at the clinic."

"I'll get the door," Troy answered, angling his chair to follow her. "See ya."

Jillian waited to hear the door lock behind her before she went back to the elevator and pushed the call button. The doors opened immediately. She pulled her keys from her pocket and stepped into the empty car with a weary sigh. Short temper and paranoia aside, LaKeytah Anthony was to be commended for keeping her home in such good shape, and for putting square meals and a strong set of values on the table every day.

As she rode the elevator down, the musty odor of age and neglect screamed for some antiseptic and air freshener. But when she stepped out into the lobby, the smell turned more perfumey, more musky, like the scent of cologne on a man.

The subtle sweetness in the air was enough to pull Jillian up short and tighten her lips into a wary frown. She turned to her right, turned to her left—held her ground as the security light over the super's door blinked on again. "Hello?"

Her breathing quickened a notch. Of course, no one would answer. The elevator had still been on the fifth floor where she and Troy had gotten out. There was no one in this lobby, no sounds beyond the usual creaks and moans of the old building, no reason for that little shiver of awareness to creep along her spine.

Get over it, girl. No one is in here spying on you.

"Right," she agreed out loud, fighting to strengthen her resolve. Seeing nothing and no one, Jillian clutched her keys like claws between her fingers, pushed open the double glass doors and hurried straight down the steps.

Long shadows cast by the high-rise buildings cooled the sidewalk as she lengthened her stride to reach her SUV. The chattering girls from the stoop across the street had gone inside. The bus stop was clear. Traffic had trickled down to a few cars. Still, that buzz of hyperawareness refused to dissipate.

She was being watched.

Whether it was idle curiosity, or something much more focused and sinister, didn't matter. Jillian tilted her head to check the windows of the apartments and businesses on either side of the street. Nothing but curtains and blinds and emptiness. It was more night than dusk now, yet she still peered into the alley across the way, looked through the windshields of the parked cars she passed. No one.

Those stupid letters had her rattled, that was all. Shivering, despite the decent warmth of the early spring evening, she jogged the last few steps to her car.

She'd just beeped the lock open when a beige Cadillac Escalade whipped around the corner and screeched to a stop beside her car, blocking her in. Instinctively on guard, Jillian drifted back a step. Had this guy been waiting for her to come out of the building?

The driver's-side window lowered and her shoulders stiffened with a flash of remembrance. And not a good one. Big black man. Shaved bald head. Muscular. Silent. Sure to be armed.

Known to her simply as Mr. Lynch.

As if she wanted to visit with a face from her past.

Get in the car!

Jillian turned and plowed right into the shoulder of a man she had even less desire to see.

"Easy, babe."

Isaac Rush.

As the whiskey-scented breath of one of Kansas City's most wily and successful drug dealers washed over her, Jillian swallowed a curse and backed away. His handsome, biracial face didn't make him charming. His tailored suit didn't make him sophisticated. The tight fingers that clamped around her elbow did make him dangerous, however.

She yanked her sleeve from his grip. "Don't call me that."

Now the big Cadillac with the armed chauffeur made sense. Jillian glanced over her shoulder and exchanged a silent nod with the big man. Lynch wasn't what she would call a friend, certainly not someone she would ever want to hang out with or run into in a dark alley, given that his job for Isaac involved guns and fists and breaking client's fingers. But, for whatever reason, the imposing, unsmiling brute had rescued her one night, a lifetime ago... from the very man who was sliding his fingers over Jillian's and the door handle right now.

But Lynch wasn't helping her tonight.

"Need something I can hook you up with, sugar?"

As if *sugar* was any better than *babe,* coming from this lowlife. Jillian snatched her hand away from the smarmy touch and stood tall. She'd be taller than Isaac if she'd been wearing heels instead of running shoes, but she doubted even that would intimidate him. "There's a reason you haven't seen me for ten years. I don't do that anymore. You have nothing I want. I was just giving a friend a ride home. Now if you'll excuse me."

Still, with money and Lynch and control of these streets to back him up, Isaac didn't give up easily. He leaned against the door, putting his body between her and getting in. "Somebody making trouble for you around here? Maybe I can help."

"You're the only trouble I see."

"Tough talk, Jilly. You know, I always liked you. And now that you're a full-grown woman, we can do something about it." *Liar!* Being seventeen hadn't stopped him from trying to *do something about* his attraction to her all those years ago. Maybe she should be grateful that his attempted rape had finally driven her to that lowest point where she could agree to entering rehab at the Boatman Clinic. But Isaac was still trying to make his role as her onetime supplier sound like something romantic had passed between them. He brushed his fingertips across the back of her knuckles. "I miss seeing you. We used to be the best of friends—"

With a silent scream pinging inside her ears, she grabbed his hand, twisted his wrist and pinched his nerve in a move her former cop brother, Eli, had taught her. Isaac yelped as his grip popped open and his knees buckled at the awkward position she'd put him in. Mr. Lynch's car door swung open, but Isaac put up his free hand to tell him to stay put.

"We were never friends." Jillian seethed between clenched teeth as she released her defensive grip and shoved him away. She pulled the SUV door open and climbed in.

"I like this new you. You've got spirit. It's hot."

With a groan at the unappreciated compliment, Jillian slammed the door shut. And locked it.

He was laughing as she started the engine. "You know where to find me if you change your mind. About anything."

Not bloody likely.

She leaned on the horn to get Lynch to move. The big black man might have saved her from some serious hurt once, had maybe even saved her life—and for that intervention she would always be grateful—but he seemed in no mood to go against his boss tonight. The time it took him to pull a cigar from his trench coat pocket and light it was the time Jillian needed to realize just how helpless she was at this moment. And just how annoyingly right Michael Cutler had been about the dangers of trespassing through No-Man's Land after dark.

Her breath caught in her throat and stuttered out on a mix of fear and adrenaline.

Locked doors couldn't keep Isaac and Lynch out if they wanted in. A bullet could pierce her windshield. They could march Troy and Dexter out here right now and threaten them, and she'd do whatever Isaac said to keep the boys safe. When she'd been high on coke or desperate for a fix, Jillian hadn't fully understood just how inescapably at the mercy of these two men she'd been.

She understood the threat now as clearly as the gun peeking from the holster inside Lynch's coat. *Get out of here!* She honked again. *Now!*

Isaac rapped on her window and grinned as she startled halfway out of her seat. "You come see me again sometime soon, babe. I'll have something real good for you, I promise. The first line will be on the house."

Then he raised his hand and signaled Lynch to move his car. The instant the Cadillac had pulled back enough for Jillian to squeeze her SUV out, she stomped on the accelerator, peeling away in a blind rush to freedom and safety, leaving Rush and Lynch and the tarnished memories from a past she couldn't quite escape behind her.

Her heart wasn't pounding so hard against her ribs that she couldn't feel the still watchful eyes glued to her every movement as she sped away.

Chapter Three

"You didn't have to call me. I'm in my room. Homework's done. I'm fine."

Despite the reassurance of the actual words, Michael Cutler heard nothing but *Go away and leave me alone* in his son's voice. He tipped his cell phone up to his temple, shifted to a more comfortable position in the cab of his heavy-duty pickup truck and breathed out a steely sigh before pulling it back to his mouth and trying again. "You want me to get some food while I'm out? I can drive through and get you a couple of burgers on the way home."

"We ate dinner."

Technically, Mike, Jr., had pushed the stew around in his bowl, eaten half his grilled cheese sandwich and rolled away from the table as fast as his wheelchair would take him as soon as Michael had granted his request to be excused. "I don't mind running to—"

"Brett's waiting, Dad."

"I see." Brett was Mike's online gaming partner. They'd once been a trio of friends—before their classmate Steve had died in the crash that had shattered Mike's legs. Now the three caballeros were down to two and Michael didn't want to see his son isolate himself from any more of his former friends. "Well, tell Brett hi. You've got postapocalyptic worlds to save, I'm sure."

"I guess. Can I go now?"

"I'll be home in time to say good-night."

"Okay."

Click.

Michael downed the last dregs of his tepid coffee and crushed the paper cup in his hand. "That went well."

About as well as a standoff with a hostage-taker who refused to negotiate.

He shoved the empty cup back into the holder between the two front seats of his black pickup. Conversations like that one were a big reason he'd been sitting outside this particular brownstone for more than an hour already. This was one problem he thought he could fix. As soon as he'd clipped his phone onto his belt, Michael pushed up the sleeve of his pullover sweater and checked the time on his military-grade watch: 8:10 p.m.

"Where the hell are you?" he whispered, turning his attention from his taciturn son to the darkened windows of Jillian Masterson's apartment building. His watch had ticked away with the same ominous slowness the night Mike hadn't shown up by curfew and he'd finally gotten a call at 2:00 a.m. from a traffic cop to tell him his son was being airlifted from the scene of an accident. He wasn't jumping to any morbid conclusions yet, but he wasn't ready to dismiss his suspicions about Jillian being in some kind of trouble, either.

A quick perusal of the building's layout told him her apartment was on the front side, facing the street where he'd parked. And though several other residents of the south Kansas City neighborhood had pulled into the adjacent parking lot, unlocked the lobby's security door and lit their windows with the warm glow of activity inside, Jillian's third-floor windows remained dark, cold and empty.

Not that it was his job to watch over the leggy physical therapist's comings and goings. But with Mike shut up inside his bedroom with his headphones on and his attention glued to the epic zombie battle he and Brett were waging online, Michael had chosen to act on a concern he *could* do something about—finding out exactly what had put the fear into Jillian's green eyes when he'd found her reading that letter in her office.

Despite the promise she made that she'd do whatever was sensible to keep herself safe, Michael's gut and the excuses Jillian had come up with to dismiss her panicked reaction were giving him the same message. Something was very, very wrong in that woman's life. He'd worked too many domestic dispute calls with his team not to be suspicious about so-called loving relationships that invoked more terror than tenderness.

What she was doing for Troy Anthony was commendable and courageous, but not reporting in after a visit to a neighborhood where gangs and drugs and prostitutes often called the shots was worrisome enough. It was downright foolish if there was some kind of unwanted admirer in her life who could use the inherent dangers of Jillian's crusade against her—or who might even be a part of that world she was trying to help Troy leave behind.

She said she'd be safe at home before dark, damn it, and the sun had set an hour ago.

He needed her to help Mike unplug himself from his isolation and anger, and move on with his life. Selfish as it might be, Michael wouldn't let her efforts to help one young man jeopardize the recovery of his own son.

Squeezing the steering wheel in his fists, Michael eased out his frustration while keeping his senses focused and sharp. He'd felt these same pangs when Pam had been consumed with cancer and was dying. He'd wanted to protect her, too—wanted to do whatever it took to drive the uncertainty from her eyes and make her smile.

Maybe he couldn't fix Mike's problems, after all.

Maybe he couldn't help Jillian.

Maybe there wasn't a damn thing he could do to help any of the people who were most important in his life.

But he'd fought for Pam until the very end—until that last evening in the hospital when she'd finally told him to let her go. He'd promised his late wife that he'd fight just as hard for their son to live a long, happy life. Thus far it seemed Michael had had more failures than success. Mike had turned to the party life to cope with his grief. In his efforts to forget the pain of losing his mother, he'd lost even more—a good friend, football, the future he'd had planned.

It would take one hell of a fight to mend his son and reclaim the close-knit family they'd once had. And if Jillian Masterson was the key…

Giving up wasn't an option.

Michael scrubbed his palm over his jaw and tried to think this situation through. He liked Jillian well enough—better than a man his age probably should. No doubt there were plenty of young bucks in K.C. who'd noticed that long, sable-colored hair and those green Irish eyes, too. He was older, not dead. Jillian's endless legs, that beautiful mouth and the sharp remarks that came out of it awakened his masculine spirit in ways he thought had died two years ago with Pam. It was hard to look into her frightened expression and not want to touch her or hold her and drive away that fear.

Ultimately, however, his feelings were irrelevant. He just had to keep Jillian safe so that she, in turn, could continue to make the miracle of Mike, Jr.'s, recovery happen.

That meant thinking like a cop—like a veteran SWAT team commander. Fortunately, that was one thing Michael *could* do without any doubts.

Did he risk a call to her brother Eli—a former KCPD internal affairs officer who now ran investigations for the D.A.'s office? Did he call one of his own men, sharpshooter Holden Kincaid, whose oldest brother, Edward, was married to Jillian's sister? In a roundabout way, he could ask if anyone had heard from her—if anyone knew of her particular plans for the evening. Did she have a meeting? A date?

"Why don't you panic the whole family and create some real chaos?" he muttered out loud. There'd be no more phone calls tonight. He knew better than that. One of the traits that made him the leader he was at KCPD was his ability to remain calm—his ability to rein in whatever he was feeling to keep his men focused and get the job done.

Michael's job tonight was simply to make sure that Jillian got home safely. Her personal life wasn't his responsibility. He just needed her in one piece and on the job Monday when he took Mike in for his therapy session. He needed Jillian to make his son smile. And laugh. And truly want to live again.

He'd ignore the stirrings in his blood teasing him that spending time with Jillian Masterson made *him* feel like living again, too.

JILLIAN STUFFED A FRENCH FRY into her mouth and reached across the seat for another as she slowed her SUV and pulled into the parking lot of her building. She circled around once, looking for an empty spot, preferably one close to the door since the rest of her day had totally sucked and the idea of braving the long, lonely parking lot by herself was about as appealing as the sensation of having unseen eyes on her 24/7.

"Great," she muttered, reaching the end of the lot and circling around again. "Just great."

When she reached the entrance again, she pulled into the only empty spot she'd seen. It wasn't terribly close to the door, but at least it was close to a streetlamp and she'd have some light along most of the walk to help keep real and imagined shadows at bay. She doused the headlights, killed the engine and tried to psych herself up by telling herself that her long day— from Loverboy's letter to running into Isaac Rush after getting bawled out by Troy's grandmother, from lusting after Michael Cutler to the need for an N.A. meeting—was almost over.

The handful of fries she'd eaten since leaving the drive-through window at a fast food restaurant sat like rocks in her stomach. Still, all her training as an athlete, physical therapist and recovering addict demanded she get some kind of nourishment into her system, no matter how tired she was. So she grabbed the bag and climbed out. Greasy dinner, sleeping in a blue and pink bedroom and finally getting to a new day wasn't much, but it *was* something to look forward to.

The beep of her remote locking the car couldn't mask the slamming of a car door nearby. The instantaneous thump of her heart couldn't drown out the crunch of approaching footsteps, either.

Jillian spun around. Where was her company? Would she recognize a neighbor? Or was it *him?*

"Hey, Jilly," the male voice drawled, stopping her at the rear of her SUV. "I've been waitin' for you."

Seeing the familiar handsome face and spiked blond hair transformed her fear into irritation. "Blake. You scared the daylights out of me. What are you doing here? Didn't you get my message?"

"Didn't you get mine?" He loosened his tie and unhooked the collar of his striped shirt. "You stood me up tonight. I thought we were having drinks."

"I never said yes to a date. I never will."

"I love a woman who plays hard to get." He leaned in close, as if he intended to kiss her, and Jillian jerked away. He clamped his hand down on her wrist and she stomped on his instep. With a howl and a curse, he instantly released her. "Maybe not that hard, baby."

Another car door slammed. Could this night get any worse?

It could.

She saw the drop of dried blood at the corner of Blake's aquiline nose and realized there was a slur to his southern drawl. She shoved him away when he leaned in again. "Oh, my God, Blake—are you using?"

"Just a little. I don't know how many times I can let you break my heart without putting a stop to it. It dulls the pain."

"It dulls the brain. You're throwing your fortune away, maybe even your career. Don't blame me for your addiction. Good night."

He shifted his stance, blocking her path when she tried to move around him. He laid his hand over his heart. "You hurt me, Jilly. Nobody's ever been able to take your place. I can get clean. I've done it before. Just give me a chance. Don't hurt me like this."

Fine. He wanted to talk pain?

"Did you send me a rose this week, Blake? Are you trying to rekindle something with me?"

"Hell, I'll buy you two whole dozen if it'll get you to come back to me."

"Did you send the flower?" She was beginning to think the answer was no, that the more expensive, dramatic gesture he'd just offered would be more his style. Still, she needed to be clear. "We are never getting together again. I told you that two Christmases ago when we tried to recapture the magic we once had."

Turned out it wasn't magic at all, but a curse. She had to have been high herself to think she'd ever been in love with a man like him.

"You need to go home, Blake, and sleep this off. In the morning, call Dr. Randolph at the Boatman Clinic. I've given you his number before. Get help. Please."

"Say you love me and I will."

MICHAEL STRETCHED HIS LONG LEGS out beneath the dashboard to control the restlessness inside him. Chances were, Jillian would show up safe and sound any minute now, and he was doing all this worrying for nothing.

Or not.

Hidden in the darkness of the truck's interior, he recognized her dark blue SUV as it zipped into the parking lot and circled around twice before she pulled into a space right next to the entrance and abruptly cut the engine and lights. In the circle of light cast by the streetlamp across from him, he could easily make out her jerky movements as she checked in every direction before grabbing a sack of takeout food from the passenger seat and locking the door behind her. Her long strides took her to the back of her SUV and she disappeared from sight.

And then he saw the blond man in the suit climb out of his Jaguar the next row over and stumble toward Jillian.

Michael's gaze narrowed. His pulse raced. "What the hell?"

He was out of his truck and dashing across the street when he heard the man shout out a curse. Michael slowed his steps, assessed the scene. Was Jillian in danger?

"Oh, my God, Blake—are you using?" Whatever was happening, Jillian seemed to be fighting the battle just fine on her own. Still, he'd seen such fear in her eyes that morning. If this was the guy responsible for putting it there…

Stepping into the grass to approach in stealth mode, Michael reached the hood of her SUV and identified each of their positions at the rear of the vehicle.

"Get help. Please."

"Say you love me and I will."

Michael circled around in time to see the blond man reach for Jillian. He snuck up behind the fool and had him in a headlock and on the ground before his fingers ever touched her.

"Michael!"

"What the hell?"

"KCPD, pal. Put your hands on your head and stay on the ground if you know what's good for you." He straightened to find Jillian staring at him, her soft mouth agape, her green eyes wide and confused. "You okay?"

"Where did you…? How did you…?" She blinked, and he read suspicion instead of gratitude there. "Are you following me?"

"This guy apparently is." The *guy* squirmed, tried to get up. Michael put a boot squarely in his back and pushed him back down to the asphalt. He still needed an answer. "Did he hurt you?"

"No. He's an old boyfriend. He wouldn't…" She hugged the sack she carried up to her chest and glanced down at the man on the ground. "His name's Blake Rivers. I just wanted him to leave me alone."

Blake Rivers tried to turn his face up to Michael. "Who are you, old man? You can't be her daddy, 'cause he's dead."

Jillian gasped. Michael knew enough of her history to know that that had been a cruel, tactless thing to say. "I'm a friend. One who's going to do whatever the lady tells me to do. Get the hint?"

He didn't. "Jilly and I have history."

"History's in the past. I'm talking about right now." Michael pressed a little harder with his boot. "Jillian, do you want this man around?"

The sack took a beating from her wringing fingers. "Blake, I told you I can't see you anymore. I just wanted to know if you had sent me a rose last week."

"Baby, I told you to your face how I feel."

"You *can't* have me back. Ever. I don't know how many different ways I can say it—you're not good for me. Now go home."

"Why? So you can bang this old fart?"

"Michael isn't—"

"Michael can handle himself just fine." Proving he was as good as his word, Michael hauled Blake to his feet and escorted him back to his car. "The lady said goodbye. You're leaving." He stopped long enough to open the car door and look him straight in the eye. "You sober enough to drive, pal?"

Blake sputtered for a moment, blinked his vision clear and then climbed into his Jaguar and started the engine. Michael was already calling in the name, plate and location to alert traffic patrol as the car pulled out and sped away.

Hopefully, he'd get home without incident. Hopefully, Michael had done enough to keep him away from Jillian.

But if he'd been expecting gratitude, or even a friendly hello, from her, he'd been mistaken.

As he rejoined her at her SUV, he didn't bother asking if she'd been rattled by the encounter with her ex. Jillian stood tall and strong. And she was spitting mad.

"Did you follow me uptown to Troy's apartment, too?"

He pointed to his pickup across the street. "No, I've been waiting over there."

Anger twisted into confusion. "That wasn't you watching me?"

"No, that jackass in the Jaguar…" She wasn't talking about now. His gaze narrowed in on the tight lines of strain bracketing her mouth and every muscle in him tensed, instantly on guard. It wasn't anger that had her so tense. "Watching? Explain."

"Never mind, Captain." She turned away.

They were back to *Captain?*

"Jillian, did something else happen?" He reached for her arm, touched the soft fleece of her sleeve.

She whirled around and smacked his hand away. "Don't touch me!"

As instantly apologetic as she'd been quick to attack, Jillian reached out and patted his chest. She smoothed imaginary wrinkles in his sweater and blood surged to the point of contact. "I'm sorry. Long day. I…" Her gaze following her shaky fingers, she brushed her fingertips over the brass and blue enamel badge clipped to his belt. If she was worried about assaulting a police officer, or muttered one word about not respecting her elders… But she curled her fingers into her palm and the explanation died in her upturned eyes. "Thank you for coming to my rescue. Sorry I hit you."

He was a man. He was a cop. He was here. He could handle whatever she had to say. Michael softened his voice, taking the authoritative clip from his tone. "Don't apologize. Just talk to me."

"I can't." Shaking her head, she wrapped both hands around the crumpled takeout sack. "You're not here to solve my problems." A tiny frown dimpled the smooth, tanned skin of her forehead. "Why are you here, anyway? Is Mike okay?"

"Mike's fine. He's holed up in his room and won't have a civil conversation with me, but I know he's safe. You? I'm not so sure."

"Just don't give up on Mike—keep trying to connect, no matter how rude or sullen he gets. You never know when the message is going to kick in. If he keeps hearing the words and seeing the actions, he'll understand that you love him, and that he's not in his fight all alone.

Well, if you don't need anything else…" She held up the fast food sack. "Dinner's getting cold."

"Sage advice, Obi-Wan. But like I said, you're the one I'm worried about right now."

"I'm okay." With a smile he didn't buy, Jillian bade him good-night and headed down the walk toward the front door again. She was on the first step when she turned to face him. A deep, ragged breath lifted her shoulders. "Who am I kidding? Would you do me a favor? If you're not on duty—of course you're not on duty, you're not in uniform—but if you don't have to be anywhere—"

"What is it?" He was already closing the distance between them. Michael stopped on the step below her, tilting his chin ever so slightly to look up into her eyes.

"Would you…" Her fingertips danced just above his chest again, as if he needed to be soothed before she could ask him the favor. His pulse seemed to pick up the same jumpy rhythm. "Would you walk me up to my apartment, Captain? Just make sure it's clear to go inside. I've had some weird things happen lately, and I'm getting a little paranoid."

More weird than that letter? "What did Blake Rivers say to you?"

"You know I used to be like him. I suppose now I'm just sober enough to know that something isn't right."

He knew she didn't talk about her past life much, but she'd shared enough. He'd have done his homework on the woman responsible for his son's recovery, anyway. And besides, Mike's response to her was so strong, it didn't make a difference. "You don't deserve this harassment. You beat your addiction, Jillian. You made something of your life."

"Not enough, it seems." Or else she wouldn't have some creep making her startle at a man's unexpected touch? "You sure you still want to help me?"

Michael simply nodded, stepping up behind her to shield her from unseen eyes she thought were *watching* as she unlocked the door and led him inside. When she hesitated at the open elevator doors, Michael touched the small of her back and guided her inside. When the doors closed behind them and she didn't move away, he let his fingers slide beneath her jacket to rest just above her belt in an even more protective gesture. The sinuous curve of her hip beneath her knit top told him she was as firm and fit as she looked.

But the pulsing heat that warmed his fingers

even at that innocent contact warned him that his interest in helping Jillian might not be as paternal and altruistic as he might have thought. He quickly drew his hand away as if he'd crossed a forbidden line of friendship and tucked his errant fingers into the front pockets of his jeans.

She'd asked the KCPD *captain* to escort her upstairs, not the red-blooded forty-four-year-old who couldn't seem to keep his hormones in check tonight.

He peered down the third-floor hallway before he let her exit the elevator. Clear. The muffled sounds of television shows and lively conversations filtered through his ears as they passed by her neighbors. Nothing unusual there. Once they reached Jillian's door, Michael put a hand on her shoulder to hold her back so he could enter her apartment first.

"No sign of forced entry," he stated as she pulled out her key. Still… Michael pressed Jillian back against the wall beside the door frame and looked her straight in the eye. "Stay put. I don't want to mistake your movement for something or someone else."

Jillian looked straight back and nodded.

Unhooking the cover on the holster at his waist, Michael rested his hand on the butt of his

Glock and crossed the tiny dining area to see what was on the other side of the counter that divided the open kitchen area. A few dirty dishes in the sink, a wireless phone on the wall with a blinking red light indicating four messages. But nothing seemed out of place. He checked the window that opened onto the fire escape off the kitchen. New lock. State-of-the-art. "Have you had a recent break-in?" he questioned.

"No. I asked Eli to replace the old lock for me. The metal had rusted."

Beefing up the locks—evidence of a woman who lived alone in the city showing common sense? Or did Jillian have a more specific reason for not feeling secure in her own home? How many *love* letters did a woman have to receive before she felt compelled to change the locks and have a cop walk through her place?

Scanning quickly and thoroughly from left to right, he moved through each of the remaining rooms. Living room clear. Bathroom clear. Her bedroom was a little messy—the smell of fresh paint tinged the air, and the bed was still rumpled from where she'd lain among the sheets and quilt. The window, inaccessible from outside without a fire engine ladder or rappelling rope, was cracked open to help disperse the paint fumes, but the room and closets were clear.

"I don't see anything out of place." Michael secured his gun and came back into the living room.

"Thank you." Jillian's shoulders sagged with genuine relief before a bolt of internal energy fired through her. She opened the door and flashed him a smile that surely meant goodbye. "You won't tell Eli or my sister that I'm losing it, will you? They worry enough about me living on my own. Now I can tell them that the finest of Kansas City's finest said there was nothing to worry about."

That wasn't what he'd said, and Michael wasn't ready to be dismissed just yet. He braced his hands on his hips and stood his ground. "Does this paranoia of yours have anything to do with that love letter you threw away this afternoon?"

Boom. Smile gone. The door drifted shut as she stormed across the apartment to meet him in the kitchen. "You went through my trash?"

Michael shrugged off the accusation. "Didn't need a warrant to do it. Something was...*is* clearly bugging you. And don't tell me it's my imagination. I know what brave people who are trying to hide how scared they are look like. Is it an abusive boyfriend? That Rivers guy who won't take no for an answer?"

She tossed the sack onto the counter and

planted herself in front of him, matching his stance and nearly matching his height. "One, I don't have a boyfriend, and two, what business is it of yours who follows me or sends me things I don't want?"

Whoa. "You were followed tonight? I told you to drive straight to a police station—"

"You're twisting my words around—"

"*You're* the one who asked me to check out your apartment." One beat of silence passed. Then another. Michael's burst of temper squeezed into something much more controlled, much more concise. "You're being stalked, aren't you?"

The flush of defensive anger drained from her face, leaving Jillian's smooth skin an alarming shade of pale. *Swift negotiating tactic, Cutler.*

When her gaze dropped to the middle of his chest and her head bobbed with a reluctant nod, it wasn't victory at finally getting a straight answer he was feeling. The nagging burn in his gut that had told him something was wrong wasn't eased one bit by the truth.

"Jillian…" Michael reached out to brush aside the strand of hair that had fallen across her cheek. He gently tucked it behind her ear, then cupped his hand against her jaw. The cool velvet of her skin, the warm beat of her pulse throbbing beneath his fingertips—*they* eased the guilt and worry in his gut. He tipped her face back up to his and drifted half a step closer. "You jump every time I enter the room, and you go on the attack every time I even suggest that you might be in danger. Sure signs you're hiding something. This isn't something you can fight on your own. You shouldn't have to."

Her nostrils flared as she took a deep breath. Her eyes locked on to his. Her hands curled into tight fists and rested against him. "I don't know what to do. I don't know how to make it stop."

Michael stroked the side of her neck, dipping his fingertips into the coffee silk of her hair. Her pulse was quick but steady. "Have you reported him to the police?"

She tapped at his chest. "And tell them what? He hasn't threatened me in any way. He just…*loves* me."

"Does it feel like love?"

Her answer was to walk straight into his chest. She clutched a fistful of the sweater she'd smoothed so meticulously earlier, and buried her face at the juncture of his neck and shoulder. She was shaking.

Michael was much more than a cop standing

there in Jillian's kitchen as he wrapped his arms around her and hugged her tight against his body, trading solace for the tactile reassurance of her warmth and trust. He turned his mouth to the delicate shell of her ear. "Now tell me who this bastard is—and why he's got you so spooked."

Chapter Four

Jillian burrowed into Michael's unyielding strength, drawing in deep breaths of the clean, musky scent that clung to his skin and the white T-shirt that peeked out above the neckline of his sweater. The overwhelming onslaught of frustration and helplessness, loosed by Michael's unexpected tenderness, calmed as the strong, steady rhythm of his heart drummed beneath her hand.

His fingers tunneled beneath her ponytail, gently massaging the tension at her nape. He slipped his arm beneath her jacket to catch her more closely around the waist, creating an intimate rustle of denim against khaki as his sturdy thighs rubbed against hers. The hardness of his gun and badge poked into her belly, but she had no desire to adjust her stance for fear the slightest movement would end the embrace.

"Have you reported this?" he whispered against her hair.

"No." She didn't want to talk. She simply wanted to breathe easy for a few moments while his strong arms and soft, deep voice shut out the chaotic events and irrational fears of the past few weeks. She just wanted to feel…safe.

And for the first time in weeks, she did.

But Michael Cutler had KCPD running through his blood, and the respite couldn't last. He wanted answers and demanded action. Tucking a finger beneath her chin, he nudged her face up to meet his probing gaze. "Your brother is married to the commissioner. Your sister is married to a homicide detective. Have you told any of them what's going on?"

Reluctantly, Jillian pushed away and hugged her arms in front of her, trying to hold on to some of his warmth. "You want me to embarrass all of them by sounding like a whack job?"

"Besides the fact that they're family and I know they care about your well-being—what if this creep has something to do with their position in the department, or a case one of them has worked on? It wouldn't be the first time a criminal has targeted a family member out of retribution. You know you should report a stalker. They'd want to know that."

Jillian shrugged, knowing just how foolish she'd sound if her story made it onto a police blotter. *Former juvenile delinquent who nearly ruined her family eleven years ago is at it again. Can't the commissioner's husband and KCPD's assistant medical examiner keep their little sister out of trouble?* "There haven't been any threats. Certainly nothing specific against my family. All I have are a handful of letters and a dead rose—"

"And the feeling that someone's following you."

"And what do I say? Hey, Eli and Holly—this guy says he loves me." Jillian picked up her cold sack of dinner and tossed it into the trash beneath the sink. What little appetite she'd had was long gone. "He might need to have his head examined, but you can't arrest a man for that."

She was beginning to wonder if the connection she'd felt with Michael—the shared heat, the need, the attraction that was growing more difficult to ignore by the minute—had all been the ruse of a skilled SWAT negotiator, to get her to drop her guard and lure her into talking. Because he was keeping his distance and the questions kept coming. "You don't know who sent that letter today?"

"I don't know who sent any of them."

"Plural?"

Why not? Whatever his reasons might be,

Michael Cutler wanted to hear her story. And she'd reached the point where she needed to tell it.

"Here." Jillian crossed into the living room and pulled out a manila envelope from the desk behind the sofa. As he'd followed her, she only had to turn around to hand him the package. "There are eight of them. They started coming about a month ago. Kansas City postmark, no return address, no name. I don't know what they'll prove, but when you've grown up around cops—"

"You hold on to potential evidence." He unhooked the flap and used the hem of his sweater sleeve to pull the first one out. "Self-gummed envelopes and stamps, so no DNA. No handwriting to trace. Probably no finger-prints, either, if he's being that careful, but I'll pull in a favor at the lab and ask them to run these for trace, anyway." His stern expression never wavered as he skimmed through the contents of each message. "Anything about the wording sound like someone you know?"

"Not really. He keeps everything pretty generic." Just personal enough to send a chill down her spine. Jillian stuck her hands into the pockets of her sweatshirt jacket and wondered if she was ever going to feel warm on her own again. "Compliments. Poetry. Promises. I call him Loverboy, but trust me, it's not an endearing nickname. I needed something tangible where I could focus my…" Fear? Loathing? Terror? Jillian shrugged. "If I knew the guy, I might think the messages were dorky, but flattering."

"Like a kid with a crush?"

"Like a sicko with a grand, idealized notion of what I'm looking for in a relationship."

"He's put you on a pedestal." Michael tucked the letters carefully back into the envelope. "I'm guessing it's someone you know, even peripherally, someone from your present or past. You've smiled at him or spoken to him or done something for him that he interprets as you having feelings for him."

"Believe me, I don't." Jillian paced back into the kitchen and filled the kettle on the stove to fix some hot tea. There had to be a way to shake the chill that filled every pore.

Michael followed. "I've answered more calls than I'd care to count because a man doesn't have a good grasp on what the reality of loving a woman is."

She froze with the box of tea bags in her hands. "Calls? As in SWAT team calls? You think it could escalate into something that serious?"

"I'm not willing to treat this as a joke. And even if you think this could be a harmless prank that would end up embarrassing your family, my years of experience tell me to consider this guy a serious threat until he proves otherwise."

Jillian turned off the stove and sank into one of the chairs at her kitchen table. Hot tea wasn't going to help. "Now you're really scaring me. What if he tries something when I'm with a patient? Or he hurts someone here in my apartment building?"

"Look, I hope I'm wrong, but in my job you're better prepared if you understand the worst that could happen. I just want you to see this in a sensible way, and take the precautions necessary to keep yourself safe. Telling me is the first step." He laid the envelope on the table and pulled out the chair beside her. When he rested his calloused fingers over hers, Jillian turned her hand and latched on to the comfort he provided. "Things could be escalating already. First, he's merely sending you notes. Now he's watching you—getting closer to actually interacting with you? What made you think he followed you tonight?"

"A movement out of the corner of my eye or a scent or I don't know what made me think I had somebody's attention when I was in Troy's neighborhood." Isaac Rush and his lieutenant, Mr. Lynch, might have topped the list as an in-her-face danger, but Isaac was hardly the love letter type—not when he could use bribery or blackmail or brute force to get what he wanted from a woman. No, this had been something more secret—more sinister—because it lived in the shadows. "I…ran across some people I knew…when I was younger."

"What people?"

My former supplier and the enforcer who saved me from being raped by said dealer one night.

Jillian's fingers twitched with the self-conscious shame she still carried with her. Michael Cutler didn't know what she'd done as a teen, who she'd been. Since she'd been a juvenile at the time, her court appearances as both the accused and accuser had been sealed. Her journey back to sobriety was her business—news that she'd once been a coke addict would probably end this conversation and his concern right now—and jeopardize Michael's willingness to let her work with his son. She chose her words carefully. "Blake is an old boyfriend, who got me into the party scene when I was in high school. I rebelled big time after my parents died. Some of those parties ended up in No-Man's Land."

She sought out his dark blue eyes, wondering if he could piece together the truth, wondering if she'd see judgment there. Nothing. No pity, no condemnation—no understanding or forgiveness, either. Just a cop with an unreadable expression.

Her fingers twitched inside his grasp. "That was my old life, Cap…Michael. I swear I'm not that person I was in high school anymore."

"Maybe this guy doesn't know that. Can you get me a list of all the men you've ever dated? Starting with those party boys in high school?" He squeezed her hand before releasing her and pulling out his wallet. When he pushed to his feet and handed her his KCPD business card, Jillian wondered if this was his answer to her vague confession. He wasn't the kind of man to be attracted to a rebellious wild child. But he would be kind and professional to anyone who needed his help—even a handful of past and potential trouble like her. "Call me if you think of anything else, or you feel like you're being followed again, whatever—day or night, you call. If anything else happens, we're making an official report. I'm not afraid to look like a fool if it turns out to be nothing."

Yeah, but he had a stellar reputation to back him up. No one would dare question Michael

Cutler's sensibility or fire up the rumor mill about a past life coming back to give him just what he deserved.

With his card in hand, Jillian followed him to the door. She hated to see him go, but had no grounds to ask him to stay. "I only wanted you to check my apartment for goblins and perverts. I wasn't asking you to launch a full-blown investigation."

Michael paused in the open doorway and turned. "I only wanted you to help my son walk again. I didn't realize I'd be asking you to heal his spirit as well. It's the most important job in the world right now, as far as I'm concerned. If I can help my go-to woman get the job done with Mike, then I intend to."

Go-to woman. She liked that. She wasn't about to let him down. "I don't mind. Mike's a cool kid."

"That he is." His gaze skimmed over her lips, and Jillian felt the brief but focused interest as intimately as a caress. "I like it when you smile. I like it a hell of a lot better than…" He blinked, and when he opened his eyes, his attention had shifted and the heat had vanished. "I don't want you distracted by this guy, Jillian. And I sure as hell don't want you hurt. Mike lost his mom, lost a friend—nearly lost his own life—in a span of two years. I don't think he could handle another blow like losing you right now."

With that charge reminding her that Jillian's mission was to help the son and not lust after the father, she pulled her shoulders back and re-assured him—reassured herself. "This guy will lose interest, and it will all blow over soon, I'm sure. Mike won't have to worry about anything. I'll be there for him."

"And I'll be here for you." He held up the manila envelope, firmly dismissing any linger-ing misconception that some sort of personal bond between them had been acknowledged and awakened tonight. "I'll call you if I find out anything about Loverboy."

"Good night, Michael. And thanks."

After she locked the door and hooked the security chain, Jillian headed back to the kitchen. Her stomach growled in protest at being forgotten since her lunch break at noon, but she was so drained by the assault on her emotions tonight that she lacked the energy to do more than grab a slice of cheese and a bottle of water from the fridge. Once the provolone had been gobbled down, she pressed the button on the answering machine and let the messages play while she peeled off her jacket, untucked her top and made her way back to her bedroom.

She shook her head as Dylan Smith's voice gasped about failing the hot pepper test, and took note of her brother, Eli, informing her that he'd be out of town for a few days while he traveled to Illinois to interview a prisoner for one of the D.A.'s cases. Yes, she had his cell number. Yes, she had Holly and Edward's number if she needed something while he was away. She cringed as Blake Rivers invited her to meet him for drinks at nine to discuss why she didn't want to see him anymore, and smiled as Dr. Randolph called to see if everything was all right. No doubt he'd gotten word that she'd stopped off at the clinic to attend a Narcotics Anonymous meeting this evening. After the unsettling letters and a run-in with Rush and Lynch, she'd needed a dose of support and a reminder that she had the power to cope with the stress in her life.

She turned on the light, tossed her jacket onto the bed and froze.

"Michael?" She mouthed the word like a prayer.

She was surrounded by cool, icy blue. There was no hot-pink wall left for her to finish this weekend. Every wall had been freshly painted, neatly trimmed. But not by her.

"Michael?" Sense. Security.

Fear tried to jump-start her feet into backing out of the room, but her eyes were drawn with morbid fascination to the mussed-up bed and dented pillow. The same bed she meticulously made every morning of her life, the way she'd been trained to do in rehab.

Her water bottle bounced across the carpet. "Michael!"

Jillian ran through her apartment, unlocked the door, cursed the chain that refused to cooperate with her jerky fingers. "Michael!" she screamed.

Once she slid the chain out of its slot, she threw open the door and sprinted down the hallway.

"Michael! Michael!"

"Jillian?" Michael's voice boomed from the stairwell. Footsteps pounded each step. "Jillian!"

"Michael!"

Seconds later he materialized at the end of the hall. Tall. He took the last flight of stairs in three strides. Dark. The expression on his face meant serious business. Dangerous. Gun drawn, charging straight ahead.

Jillian flew into his arms and clung tight around his neck. "He was in my apartment. He was in my bed."

"YOU'RE CERTAIN IT WAS THE SAME GUY who did this?" Detective Edward Kincaid scribbled a detail on his notepad. The paint roller was conveniently missing and the paint can in her closet had been pristinely cleaned.

Jillian hugged her arms hard around her waist, still feeling a creepy sense of violation just standing in the doorway to her bedroom. "Unless you or Eli came in and worked, and then lay down on my bed for a nap, I'm sure there's no one else who would have painted this today."

"Easy, kiddo. I'm pretty sure my partner will alibi me for today." He braced his hand on his knee and pushed to his feet.

"You know I wasn't accusing you."

"I know." Jillian's brother-in-law was a big, scarred-up man, a little on the quiet side unless he had something important to say—and he took very seriously his role as stand-in big brother while Eli was out of town.

After pocketing his notepad and pen, he turned Jillian away from her bedroom and, limping ever so slightly beside her on his rebuilt knee, walked her back into the living room. "So what do I tell Holly about this Cutler guy?"

"I thought you were here to take my statement."

He scrubbed a hand over his scarred chin and jaw while she took a seat on the sofa. "Not grill you on your personal life?"

Jillian's gaze darted over to Michael, speaking in a hushed, articulate tone on his cell in her kitchen. He was probably on the phone to Mike, Jr., explaining why he was so late coming home. "Captain Cutler isn't part of my personal life. I work with his son at the clinic."

The cushion beside her sank as it took Edward's weight. "Uh-huh." He closed his hand over both of hers where they rested in her lap. "And that's why you were holding on to him so hard when I showed up. Cutler's lucky he's got any hands left the way you were wringing on his."

"Edward."

"Look, you know I've got your best interests at heart. Holly's going to freak when I tell her you had a break-in at your place. Imagine what she'll do when she finds out there's a new boyfriend in the picture, too."

"He's not a boy."

"Interesting distinction to make." He waved aside any attempt to reword her protest. "Kiddo, you've got the oldest soul of anybody I know—except me, maybe. And we all know what a jackass your last date, Blake Rivers, turned out to be. I get why you'd be drawn to a mature man like Cutler."

"You make him sound like he's over-the-hill." Despite the shards of silver in his hair, she knew from very personal contact that Michael Cutler was fit and firm and strong in every way a man should be. With his badge out to warn curious neighbors back into their apartments, he'd carried her all the way down the hallway to her apartment with one arm around her waist. And he hadn't let go until she'd buzzed Edward into the building forty-five minutes ago. "He's not."

Edward squeezed her hands. "Hey, I'm not judging your taste in men. Your sister fell for a beat-up piece of work like me, and I thank God every day she did. I just don't want to see you have any more hurt in your life."

"Holly fell for you because you were there for her when she needed a hero. Michael's just a friend who wants me to help his son. I've got a stupid crush on him, that's all."

"Whatever you say." Edward leaned in and teased, "He breaks your heart, I break his legs. Even if he does outrank me."

"Edward!" Jillian smacked his shoulder with a sisterly jab and laughed.

"I haven't heard that sound for a while." Michael flipped his phone shut as he joined them. Good grief! Jillian's cheeks burned at the idea he might have overheard exactly what

they'd been discussing. But if he had, he
politely overlooked her misguided feelings and
stuck to cop speak with Edward. "Investigat-
ing's not my specialty, but I do know a thing or
two about surveillance and protection. I called
in some members of my team who'll take shifts
to keep an eye on the apartment building so we
can start documenting who comes and goes,
maybe have a chat with anyone who doesn't
belong. I'll see if I can arrange regular drive-
bys at the physical therapy clinic next week,
too."

"I'll get the ball rolling from my end, then—
get the history we have so far documented in
the system. At the very least we've got a
crackpot with no respect for personal space,
and at the worst…"

He didn't need to finish that sentence. Jillian
knew her brother-in-law had seen the worst life
had to offer. She knew her sister's love had
brought him back from the brink of losing
himself to an addiction the same way she had.
He squeezed her shoulder before standing.
"The first order of business is changing your
locks. There are no signs of forced entry, so that
means somebody has a key."

"But Holly and Eli are the only ones I gave
a key to."

Michael splayed his fingers at his hips, his gun and badge and guarded stance reflecting something more than the warrior-like persona she was used to seeing in the other men in her life. "It's easy enough to make a copy if someone can get his hands on the key."

That something extra was an air of command that even big, bad Edward deferred to. "The building super will be my first stop on the way out." He glanced down at Jillian. "Who else might have access to your keys?"

It was rare for Jillian to feel short and small, but being flanked by the twin towers of testosterone was a little disquieting. So she asserted her own strength and stood. "I wear them on my wrist at work, or since I don't usually carry a purse, I stuff them in my pocket. I think they're still in my jacket."

"Get them so I can have the lab check for tool marks or any other signs of tampering—and pack a bag with whatever else you might need. You can stay out at our place tonight. I'll make sure the lock gets rekeyed first thing tomorrow morning." He flicked a glance over to Michael, then came back to read her face as well. "If you haven't already made other plans?"

Michael's dark blue eyes were already locked on to hers when she lifted her gaze to

his. That look made her feel important, pro-
tected. *He* made her feel safe. Not new locks.
Not the entire force at KCPD seemingly now
at her disposal with these two cops reporting
the break-in. A ridiculously idealistic thought
crossed her mind. Wrapped up in Michael's
arms, breathing in the scent and strength that
was uniquely his—*that's* where she felt safe.
For a woman who had guarded her heart and
denied the impulses of her own feminine needs
for so long, the urge to reach out to Michael and
get closer to him in whatever way she could
was suddenly so potent within her that her
fingers drummed nervously together and she
had to shove her hands into her pockets to keep
them at her side.

Michael had a teenage son at home that he
wouldn't want to endanger. Besides, they were
friends. *Just friends.* She couldn't ask him to do
any more for her than he already had. She
blinked, and the needy spell was broken. "No,
I haven't made plans."

Michael's eyes shuttered and he circled
around her to shake Edward's hand. "You'll get
those letters to the lab?"

Edward nodded. "I'm glad you were here,
Captain. If that bastard had still been in here
when she got home…"

"I'd have taken him out," Michael stated matter-of-factly, releasing his hand. "You keep her safe."

"Yes, sir."

Michael had his hand on the doorknob when he stopped, turned and strode back across the room. Edward must have discreetly stepped aside, because suddenly Michael Cutler was in Jillian's space, his dark eyes narrowed as he skimmed every nuance of her startled, hopeful expression. With just his fingertips, he brushed her hair off her face and tucked it behind her ear. Leaving his fingers tangled in her hair, he shaped his hand to cup her jaw. And then he leaned in, his lips aiming for her cheek, but hovering just short of making contact.

Jillian held her breath as his chest expanded and contracted with a weary sigh that tickled across her skin. With the subtle pressure of his fingers, he angled her face, lowered his head and covered her mouth with his own.

The kiss was hard, unapologetic, and achingly abrupt with everything she sensed he was holding back. Jillian's blood heated in an instant response and her lips softened, parted, wanted. She leaned in.

But the kiss was over and Michael was

leaving before she'd barely braced her hand against his chest.

He pulled away, walked away, opened the door. "I'll see you Monday at the clinic."

Her brother-in-law's voice startled her from her prolonged stare at the door Michael had closed behind him. "You sure what you're feeling is one-sided?"

Jillian was no longer sure of anything tonight. "I'll go pack my bag."

THE ELEVATOR BUTTON DINGED.

Ignoring her broken moans the way he'd ignored her wasted pleas, he pulled the old woman out of the shadows and dragged her onto the elevator. He pressed the number 5 button, then stepped over her and walked out of the building into the night. The unscrewed bulb over the super's door had never once given him away.

After climbing into his vehicle, he pulled out a handkerchief, wiped the blood off the brass knuckles he wore and stuffed them both back into his coat pocket. Once he was out of the neighborhood, he peeled off his gloves and tossed them into the first trash can he drove past.

His message had been clear. The old woman would never make *that* mistake again. Jillian would be safe.

He pulled down the visor above the steering wheel and smiled at the picture there. Pressing a kiss to his fingers, he reached up to stroke her dark brown hair.

"I love you, Jilly."

In every way that mattered, he would always take care of her.

Chapter Five

The weekend passed and Monday morning
dawned without further incident. No letters, no
break-ins, no kissing, no Michael. Jillian
wouldn't have thought the KCPD commander
to be the impulsive type, but how else could she
explain that kiss?

It hadn't been any paternal peck on the cheek
or kind reassurance. It hadn't been a clumsy,
inexperienced attempt to show off who the big
man was in the room, either.

Michael's kiss had felt passionate, like a man
staking his claim. Like a man hungry for something he couldn't quite put into words. His kiss
had slipped past barriers and cracked open the
door on something unnamed and unspoken
deep inside Jillian, too.

But they were *just friends*.

Her mission was to help Mike, Jr., heal—not
help herself to Mike's father. She'd done too

many selfish, hurtful things back when she'd been using, and there was a lifelong penance to pay because of it. Mike Cutler, Jr., needed her, and that's where her thoughts should be focused. Michael, Sr., was everything she hadn't fully realized she wanted in a man until now. But he was off-limits.

That kiss had been a onetime thing—an aberration her bruised heart couldn't afford to repeat.

She spent the weekend building up her confidence again and locking her protective emotional armor back into place. She let Holly pamper her with hot chocolate and late night sister-to-sister talks about everything important and nothing in particular at their rustic country home on the outskirts of Kansas City. With Edward watching over her shoulder, Jillian herself had supervised the installation of a new door lock and dead bolt for her apartment. She answered Eli's worried phone call and assured him that there was no need to cut his trip short and have the D.A. send a replacement to conduct the prisoner interview.

She didn't want her family worrying over her and curtailing their own lives the way they had when she'd been using and on and off the streets. She was an adult now. She carried a ten-year sobriety pin on her key chain. She had a master's degree and a professional career. Edward and KCPD had an investigation into the letters and break-in well under way. And she was getting to know the members of KCPD's SWAT Team 1—Michael's team—by name.

Holden Kincaid.

Rafe Delgado.

Trip Jones.

Alex Taylor.

They introduced themselves when they parked outside her building; she brought them coffee. There couldn't be a better guarded woman in all of Kansas City. Loverboy didn't stand a chance.

So why had it been impossible to sleep in her own bed last night and spend any more time than was absolutely necessary at her apartment this morning?

Jillian pressed her fingers to her neck and marked off her pulse against her watch as she started her last lap around the hospital complex. She'd gotten in early enough before the PT clinic opened to put in two miles before hitting the showers and getting ready for her first patient. What she couldn't forget about the weekend she hoped she could beat back into the recesses of her mind with a good, hard workout.

She waved to Alex Taylor, a young Latino cop who was the newest and youngest member of Michael's team. Poor guy. Low man on the totem pole got stuck with dawn patrol. He sat in the hospital parking lot in his beat-up Jeep, drinking a super-size cup of coffee and wolfing down some sort of breakfast wrap. He gave her a salute and a smile and was unwrapping a second breakfast item by the time she'd rounded the corner of the building beyond the parking lot.

Jillian was running along the exercise pathway lined with elm trees, just beginning to bud out with their leaves, when she saw that she'd have company on the last leg of her run. "Hey, Smith! So how did those hot peppers work out for you Friday?" she teased, pulling up beside her coworker and matching his pace. "Did you make the bet?"

"Morning, Masterson." Uh-oh. That didn't sound too positive.

Dylan's blond curls were sticking to the perspiration dotting his forehead and temple, indicating he, too, had been running for some time. Their positions on the exercise path must have been staggered just right for her not to notice him until now. "So, are you slowing down or am I catching up?" she asked between breaths.

"It has to be me," he drawled. "I'm still hurtin' from Friday. I did great on the first five habaneros. With my glass of milk, I thought I was going to get through all twelve. Then I sprouted a fever. My eyes watered. My toenails were sweating. By the eighth one, I was done." He buzzed his lips with a cranky sigh. "They've been burning through me ever since."

Jillian couldn't stop the grin that split her face. "I knew that was a sucker's bet."

"Hey, no laughing," Dylan whined.

"Did you get your date with Miss Hottie in Occupational Therapy?"

"Yeah, but I had to put it off until next weekend, I felt so crummy. How about you? Did you get your paint job done?"

Smile gone. Laughter forgotten. Jillian pretended the uncharacteristic hitch in her step was due to uneven pavement rather than any creepy memory of a stranger violating her apartment. Ignoring Dylan's question, she kicked her stride into a higher gear and challenged him to beat her to the finish line. "We'd better get those peppers out of your system and get you back in shape if you've got a date. Last one to the clinic cleans the stinky towels out of the locker room."

"You wish!"

She barely beat Dylan around the hospital grounds. She couldn't run fast enough to outpace her own fears.

"That's not good." Jillian slowed her steps to a jog when she spotted Alex Taylor on his cell phone, pacing outside the PT Clinic's glass doors.

"What's the scoop, Masterson?" She'd been running so hard, trying to blank out her thoughts, that she'd almost forgotten Dylan Smith had been running the path behind her. She felt his fingers sliding down the length of her ponytail until he caught a handful of her shirt and pulled her back to a cautious pace beside him. "Is he wearing a gun?"

"He's a cop." A twinge caught in Jillian's side as she abruptly stopped and sucked in deep gasps of air to catch her breath. "Officer Taylor?"

Alex cut his phone call short and moved toward her, his dark eyes fixed with a menacing light on the blond man running up behind her. "Everything cool here, ma'am?"

Did he think Dylan had been chasing her? Jillian pinched one hand at her side and held up the other to warn him off. "Friendly race, Officer," she assured him between breaths. "Dylan Smith. He works with me."

"We got a call from Dispatch, ma'am. I've

got to suit up and run." Alex Taylor was barely her height and no older than she was. Still, he conveyed a pointed look over her shoulder, silently warning Dylan that everything had better be friendly between them. "But I want to make sure everything is all right before I go."

"A call?" As in something that required guns and body armor and outthinking bad guys who didn't want to surrender? "With Captain Cutler?"

"Yes, ma'am. He'll run the team and coordinate with Bomb Squad on this."

Bomb squad? Oh, Lordy. *That* little stitch in her side had nothing to do with her vigorous run. She understood cops, understood the danger they had to face—but this morning, the true meaning of that danger hit her square in the gut. Men like Michael Cutler, like her brother, like Alex Taylor, were true warriors. They had bigger enemies to take on than her overattentive fan. The men and women of KCPD were well trained for situations just like this. Michael didn't need to be distracted by her problems. He needed to focus on the job he had to do, and gather his team around him. Now.

Feeling as if she'd already wasted too much of Alex's precious time, she waved him away toward his Jeep. "I'm fine. Go."

"I'm sure the captain will have one of us

back at your place tonight." Alex was already backing toward his car. "Just use your common sense. Try to stay with people you know. Call if you need anything."

"I will. Don't worry about me." She was a little rattled, a little winded, but more than determined to send him on his way. "Now go. Save the day. Kansas City needs you."

And watch Michael's back.

Once Alex sped away in his Jeep, Dylan laid his hand on Jillian's shoulder. "Did he say *bomb?* Why are you talking to a cop? Are you okay, Jilly? Are *we?*"

She straightened at Dylan's frantic tone. "It's nothing here. Don't worry. He's, um…doing some security work for the father of one of my patients." *Smooth way to skew the truth, girl.* She pulled her keys from the pocket of her shorts and unlocked the door ahead of Dylan. She was ready to end this conversation and get going on something useful that wouldn't give her time to worry about the dangers of Michael's job and would prove to him that she wasn't a distraction *he* needed to worry about.

Loverboy had already created enough havoc in her life. She didn't need to complicate it any further by adding her own misguided feelings about Michael Cutler into the mix.

"I've got my first patient in twenty minutes. I need to hit the showers. Stinky towels are on you, Smith."

"MIKE?" Jillian halted in the PT Clinic lobby after taking her last patient back to her room in the geriatric wing of the main hospital. Lulu had company at the front desk. "What are you doing here? I wasn't expecting you until three o'clock."

After back-to-back sessions all morning, her stomach had been set on a sandwich from the cafeteria, her mind set on catching up on some paperwork. A blue-eyed teenager with doom and gloom stamped all over his downturned features hadn't been part of the plan. "There's no school."

Spring break, right. Most kids would be celebrating.

"And you're so bored out of your mind that you came to see me?"

That taunt earned an eye roll. Good. At least now he was looking at her as she walked up to his chair to continue the conversation. "Did your friend Brett drop you off?"

"No. He's on the school trip to D.C."

For one fleeting moment, Jillian scanned the lobby and even peeked through the glass doors into the parking lot out front to see if she could get a glimpse of his father. But there was no tall, dark man in uniform, no familiar black pickup parked outside.

Mike must have sensed where her thoughts had turned. "Dad's at work. His team got called in early this morning."

"So I heard."

"Some guy's trying to rob a bank." Was Mike worried about his dad? His blasé tone said no. But then stoicism seemed to be a family trait, and Mike, Jr., was a hard son of a gun to read at the best of times. She understood how time alone at home could give a body more time to think about things he or she didn't want to think about. Maybe he was worried, and showing up for his appointment two and a half hours early was his way of showing it. Wasn't being trapped with her thoughts and fears the reason she'd gotten up at 5:00 a.m. to go running?

"Any word on what's happening?" *Whether or not anyone's been hurt?* A knot of dread soured the idea of lunch in her stomach.

"There hasn't been anything on the TV yet," Mike answered. "That's usually a good sign."

"TV is your barometer to tell how well the police are doing?"

"Hey, if Dad's not on a special news bulletin, then that means he's got it all under control."

If that wasn't the answer a cop's son would give, she didn't know what was. For both their sakes, Jillian had to laugh. And change the subject to one that wasn't quite so disquieting. "So, how did you get here? You didn't drive, did you? You know you're not allowed to do that with those braces, right?"

"If Troy can figure out the bus, so can I. I didn't know I'd get here so freaking early. You're not going to send me home and make me come back again, are you?"

Instead of teasing him about miscalculating time or the efficiency of Kansas City's public transit system, she complimented his resourcefulness. "Sounds to me like you're getting around a lot more independently than you give yourself credit for."

"Can't we just do the session now?"

"Well, you're welcome to come hang out with me anytime." A sudden inspiration twisted her thoughts into something a little more devilish. "But I've got work to do. If you're going to be here, then I'm going to put you to work, too."

"Work?" He smacked at the velcro brace on his thigh. "What can I do?"

"You'd be surprised, big guy. Come on." She unhooked the brakes on his wheelchair and turned him toward the hallway leading to the gym, workout rooms and their offices. "First things, first, though. Have you had lunch? That's where I was headed. I'll even show you the shortcut I use to get from the PT wing to the main building."

"I'm not hungry."

"I thought guys your age ate 24/7. Unless you're sleeping, of course." She nudged him a step closer into polite sociability. "My treat."

"Just a couple of cheeseburgers, I guess. I suppose eating will kill a little time."

"You sweet talker you. Is that how you charm all your dates?"

"Date? Jeez, Jillian, you're old enough to be, well, not my date. I came for a stupid PT session, that's all."

Over the hill at twenty-eight, hmm? But Jillian took no offense. Mike's blushing cheekbones indicated a healthy burst of circulation, and sitting up straighter in his chair meant he was tightening those core muscles. Jillian smiled behind his coal-black head. Score one for the PT today.

She bypassed the gym entrance and pushed Mike around the corner toward the recreation lounge, chatting away as they passed the windows and locked door of her office. "There are all kinds of hidden corridors in this complex. In some places, they built a new addition adjacent to an older part of the building, leaving these open passageways between them. Did you bring your cane?"

"I forgot." Probably on purpose. As if she'd let him sit on his duff for an entire afternoon, cane or not.

"Then I guess we're limited to wherever the chair can go. But there is this one cool place off the lounge where, if you were mobile on two feet, you could walk through without anyone knowing you're even there. It opens up in the back of the storage closet next to the pop machine and leads straight to the equipment closet off the gym. Of course, you have to have keys to get into the closets in the first place, but it's cool if I get really thirsty to just buzz from closet to closet, get a soda and sneak back in without anyone ever knowing I left."

Mike seemed intrigued by the possibilities. He pointed to the storage closet behind the tables and chairs as soon as they entered the lounge. "It'd be a sweet way to sneak up on someone and scare the crap out of 'em."

"Hadn't thought of that. I bet Lulu would jump a mile if you opened up the closet door and yelled 'Boo' while she was taking her coffee break."

"Can I look?"

"Yeah, but you can't go in with that chair." Jillian pulled her keys off her wrist and unlocked the door. Then she turned on the overhead light and picked her way through crates of soda pop cans and vending machine snacks. She pushed open the panel at the back of the closet. "See? Would you rather go exploring? Or help me clean equipment and file my reports?"

"I know what you're doing, Jillian."

She winked. "It usually works, doesn't it? Want to check it out?"

He grabbed his wheels and neatly spun himself away from the closet. "I'm hungry. Let's go get cheeseburgers."

Quickly catching up to him, Jillian guided his chair through the patio doors and along the walkway that led across a garden courtyard to the cafeteria wing on the opposite side. "Okay. But trust me, filing reports is pretty boring stuff."

Thirty minutes and three cheeseburgers later, Jillian was pushing his chair back through the lounge and down the hallway to her office. "Okay, Mike, last chance. You can choose alphabetizing files behind door number one or dishpan hands from washing the jump ropes and wiping down the free weights." She paused to unlock and push open her door, giving Mike plenty of room to roll past her into the room. "I know. There is a third option. You can put that smiling face to good use and help Lulu greet patients at the check-in desk."

His answering glare was spot-on.

"Files it is." But when Jillian would have laughed, she choked on a muffled scream instead. "What now?"

In a heartbeat, the world around her shrank down to the bouquet of twelve crimson carnations sitting in a vase on her desk. Her pulse thundered in her ears. She squeezed her keys so tightly in her fist that she nearly pierced the skin of her palm. Locked. The damn door had been locked!

Defiant curiosity drove her feet across the room for a closer look, but the fear that oozed out her pores and crept across her skin kept her from touching anything. Unlike the rose she'd received last week, this bouquet had a card attached. An unsigned card that simply read *You're welcome.*

For what? "You think I'm grateful for your help, you sick son of a—"

"Jillian? Are you talking to me?"

Mike. She wasn't alone. She whirled around, zeroed in on dark blue eyes.

"Where's your dad?" She patted her pockets,

looking for the business card Michael had given her on Friday. Maybe it was in her jacket. She pulled her running jacket off the coat stand beside the door and rummaged through the pockets. Empty. She tossed it on a hook. "Do you know your dad's number?"

"Yeah, but he's at work. It's for, you know, emergencies. You can leave a voice mail. Is something wrong? Do you need me to leave?"

She was still a bit too dazed by the violation of this latest message to know much beyond one thing right now. "I need to call Michael."

She needed to hear that deep voice and feel his calming, strengthening touch right now.

With the misfortune of impeccable timing, Dylan Smith chose that moment to show up at her door, knock and waltz right past her to her desk. He touched one bloodred flower and leaned over to sniff it. "Nice. Somebody must have been paying attention to the fact you don't like roses. You gonna let these die, too, Masterson?" He straightened and glanced over his shoulder. "That's hard on a man's ego, you know, to see how little you care about his gifts."

"I don't care about..." His teasing transformed her shock into suspicion. She wedged herself between him and the desk and, standing nose to nose, backed him up a step. "How did you know about the flowers?"

He pointed his thumb over his shoulder. "Um, passing by? Door open?"

"Did you put the bouquet in here?"

"I just got back from lunch."

She advanced. "Answer my question."

He retreated. "I saw them at the front desk and—"

"Did you put the flowers in here?" She poked him in the chest and nudged him back another step. "Do you have a key to my office?"

"No! Chill." His raised hands and irritated frown indicated she'd gone past curious interrogation. "Jeez, Jilly. I was just saying, I saw the flowers at the front desk when I went to lunch. Who put the burr up your butt today?"

"Hey, buddy, just leave her alone, okay?" Mike edged the wheel of his chair between her and Dylan.

Dylan arched a golden brow and glared at the teen. "And you are?"

"A patient, Dylan," Jillian defended. Apparently one with a protective streak that echoed his father's. She shoved her bangs off her forehead and inhaled a calming breath. Remembering that she was the adult here, she rested her hand on Mike's shoulder, thanking him and reassuring him at the same time. "I'm sorry I jumped down your throat like that, Smith. But Mike isn't the problem here. Did I tell you someone broke into my apartment on Friday?"

Dylan swore beneath his breath and was instantly contrite. "No. Did they take anything?"

"They didn't steal anything. Whoever it was got in and painted my bedroom."

"Painted…? Is that a crime?" Dylan asked.

"Someone broke in?" Mike repeated, perhaps better understanding her sense of violation. "Are you okay?"

"I'm fine. I'm just a little paranoid about my space and my things now. I don't like knowing someone was in here while I was out. I don't want these. Here." She picked up the vase and thrust it into Dylan's hands, shooing the flowers away as though they disgusted her. Bright, beautiful blooms aside, they did. At the last moment, she snatched the card from the bouquet and stuffed it into her slacks. "Would you take those down to the hospital wing for me? Maybe give them to Mrs. Carter. She was here this morning."

"That's a nice gesture, but they're so pretty… they must mean something special."

"My allergies have been acting up."

"Okay. To the hospital they go." Dylan squeezed her arm and offered a sympathetic smile. "No worries. You take care."

After Dylan had gone, Mike frowned. "You have allergies?"

"No." Jillian circled her desk. She tossed a stack of folders into Mike's lap. "Why don't you start by alphabetizing these?"

Then she pulled out the hospital directory and sat down to dial the number for Maintenance.

She'd be changing the lock on her office door, too.

Chapter Six

"Think, Cutler."

Michael muffled his helmet mike beneath his gloved hand and leaned back against the brown SWAT van where he'd set up his command post. Dale "Buck" Buckner had hung up on him again, sticking by his promise to *blow away* his ex-girlfriend and detonate the bomb he claimed to have rigged to explode the instant her limp thumb came off the detonator's trigger. What a hell of a way to terrorize someone he supposedly cared about. Her weeping pleas hadn't moved him any more than Michael's logic had.

This morning's bank robbery hadn't turned out to be about money at all. This six-hour standoff was about *love,* loss and a sheaf full of violated restraining orders.

Greedy gunmen were a cinch to negotiate with compared to a call like this one. Thieves might be desperate, but they wanted something. Michael could give them what they wanted— at least long enough for his men to take them down and put them in cuffs.

But a guy like Buckner had nothing to lose. He didn't care about his freedom. He didn't care about his life or the lives of his ex-girl-friend's coworkers. He sure as hell didn't care about material things. He just wanted his woman back. And if that didn't happen, he'd make sure that no one else could have her, either. And he'd take out anyone who tried to keep them apart—Michael, her boss at the bank, the Jackson County judicial system, pretty much anyone who made his ex laugh or smiled at her or even looked her direction. Buck thought he could force Daphne to love him and walk out of that bank a free man.

Michael knew better. This was going to end badly. Daphne Mullins was going to wind up dead and Buck would kill himself, and anyone else who happened to get in his way, so that he wouldn't have to live without her.

The waste of it all squeezed like a fist in Michael's gut. He was getting too old for this kind of crap. Too old for fighting and trying and people still dying.

God, he wanted to be young again. He

wanted to feel strong and invincible, the way he had when Jillian Masterson had walked into his arms and held on to him as though he just might have the answers she needed. He wanted to feel the hope pounding through his cynical veins again. See the trust shining in her sweet green eyes. He wanted to kiss her and touch her and come alive again, in ways he seemed to have forgotten since his wife's death and Mike's accident. The stubborn brunette with her risky do-gooding and miracle smile had turned to him as though she believed he could save the day. And for that brief moment when she kissed him back, he believed he could.

But after six hours, with only one hostage released, Michael didn't have any more answers in him. He wasn't the hero Jillian needed any more than he was the man getting the job done here.

Tuning out the chatter on the radio inside his helmet, as well as the doubts settling inside his heart, Michael tipped his chin up to the sunshine. He needed to forget about what he was feeling and clear his head. He needed options, short of storming the bank and taking out innocent hostages and maybe even losing his men in the process. Perfect blue sky. Perfect spring weather—sunny, but not too hot, even suited up in the layers of protective and communications gear and weaponry he wore. What a lousy, lousy day.

The streets outside the Drury State Bank looked as if the army were gearing up for another D-day invasion. Police cruisers, the bomb squad robot and its armored command center, uniformed cops, off-duty officers, detectives, snipers, bomb squad techs—all waited for his word to launch their attack and take out the SOB who'd walked into the bank that morning with a military duffel bag and a suicidal attitude.

Michael had tried every trick in the book. But giving up wasn't an option. His men were depending on him for guidance. Kansas City was depending on him for protection. Daphne Mullins was depending on him for her very life. He needed to calm himself, get creative, think beyond the pages of any training manual.

And then his upturned eyes zeroed in on the roof of the bank. Could that be the new trick he needed? Standard bank security had every entrance sealed tight, and Buckner wasn't about to let anyone on the bank staff override the lockdown. But what if there was a way in that didn't involve doors or windows?

Michael pushed away from the van, energized by the chancy idea that just might work if his men lived up to the speed, accuracy and resourcefulness of their training.

He tapped the microphone in his helmet and summoned his men while he organized his plan. "I need a sit rep. Who's got eyes on our perp?"

"Shades are still drawn on the front windows, boss," Holden Kincaid answered from his position on the rooftop across the street. The deep voice of Michael's number-one sharp-shooter crackled through the static in his ear. "I do not have a shot at this guy. I repeat, I do not have a shot."

Alex Taylor, the young patrol officer whom Michael had handpicked to replace Dominic Malloy, the funny man who'd been gunned down in a shoot-out at a safe house, added his obser-vations from his position at Kincaid's side. His job was to protect Kincaid and keep an ongoing assessment of potential casualties in the area so that the sharpshooter could concentrate on making his shot and taking out the perp on a moment's notice. "I've got two thermal images on the monitor on the other side of those blinds."

"But there's no way to tell which one is Buckner and which is the woman," Kincaid pointed out.

Malloy had been Holden Kincaid's best bud and a damn good scout. Taylor had some big shoes to fill, and the rest of Michael's men didn't hesitate to point that out. But to his credit, Alex Taylor didn't seem to be backing down, either. "What I was saying is that none of the other hostages are showing up on the thermal. Could be he's moved them to a separate room or into the vault."

That meant there might be a way to get them out. The brain cells were ticking.

"Trip?" Michael spoke into the mike again, summoning their big man, Joseph Jones, Jr.— Triple J or Trip, as the men liked to call him. "You still on the roof of the bank?"

"Yes, sir."

"How fast can you open the AC vent up there with the tools you've got on you?"

He heard the hesitation in Trip's voice. "The fans are still running inside. Anyone who goes through there would be chopped to bits unless we kill the power, and that would alert Buckner for sure. There's no clear path."

"How fast?" Michael repeated. If Trip could jerry-rig a truck to run on parts scavenged from a lawn mower engine, a feat he'd accomplished on a survival training mission, he could make this happen.

"I'm on it, sir." He heard the scuff of boots
or a rifle being laid on the roof as the big man
went to work. "I'm assuming you want me to
figure out a way to stop the fans, too?"

"You're reading my mind, Trip." Michael
was back at his post now, sighting each of his
men and the other KCPD men and women who
were keeping curiosity seekers and the press at
bay.

He spotted Rafe Delgado, charming a pretty
blonde reporter into staying inside her news
van beyond the cordon tape. "Delgado. Get me
something to talk to Buck about. I'm going to
call him back and keep him distracted while
Trip's working."

Rafe secured his rifle on his hip, tapped the
news van and signaled the driver to move
farther away from the potential blast area. Then
he was on the horn again, a reliable source of
information, as usual. "The heart attack victim
Buckner released is en route to Truman
Hospital. Looks like he'll make it. I've got the
name on Buckner's cell mate at Leavenworth,
where he served his time before the army dis-
charged him. The warden says he's a phone
call away if we need him. His civilian parole
officer is on the scene with me, but says he
doubts Buckner will listen to him. No luck

getting a hold of his mother, either. Looks like you're going to have to sweet-talk him out all by yourself, boss."

"You know what a charmer I can be." He allowed his men their moment of stress-relieving laughter, then got dead serious again. "Let's make this happen, men. Let's get these hostages out. That's priority one." He picked up the phone to make the call. "Trip? Tell me you've got a way in through the roof, big guy."

"Almost there, sir. Running silent is slowing me down. Just about… Oh, hell."

Michael stopped dialing. *Oh, hell* was not part of the plan. "Trip—explain."

"Little man, I need you up here."

Alex Taylor was nearly a foot shorter than Trip. "I know you are not talking to me."

"Get up here, Shrimp. My shoulders won't fit through here. I can't cut it open any further without going electric, and Buckner would be sure to hear the saw."

Taylor groaned. "You got this?"

Holden answered his new partner. "I'm good. If he cracks those blinds, I'm taking him out."

"Belay that wish, Kincaid. Wait for my signal," Michael ordered. His goal was to prevent *any* casualties, and until he knew the setup of the bomb inside, that meant getting as many innocents out of there as possible before risking the final solution. "Taylor, I want you on the roof now. I need you inside in five minutes. Preferably in one piece."

"Yes, sir."

"Delgado—I want you to rig a minicharge that will bring down that window. Then join Kincaid to back him up. That'll be your best sight line. Trip, I want you ready to go in the instant Taylor can get an access door open for you, and help him get those hostages out. I need eyes on this guy, people. I need eyes."

Michael punched in the last number and waited for Buckner to pick up on his end.

It rang twice before the man with the bomb and the gun picked up. "Yeah? What do you want now, Cutler?"

Daphne Mullins's labored breathing tore at Michael's conscience. But he tuned out her distress and focused on the job at hand. "Buck. I've got an old friend of yours here. Your P.O. He says you won't talk to him. You want to tell me why?"

Five minutes later, the answers Michael needed to hear reported in with succinct, whispered tones in his earphone. The bomb trigger taped to Daphne Mullins's thumb was a dud. The so-called explosives in Buckner's bag were nothing more than wires and laundry, according to Taylor and Trip. But the .40-caliber S & W and 9mm Glock he carried were real enough.

Ten minutes later, Buck was still haranguing away about the unfairness of a world that would keep him and Daphne apart while Alex and Trip were silently moving the hostages to the rear exit.

"Captain? The alarm's going to sound as soon as I open this back door," Trip whispered.

Michael had already pulled the phone away from his mike. "Understood. Holden? You and Delgado ready up there?"

"Yes, sir."

"On my mark, take out the window, get the hostages out the back, and Holden, take this guy down." He inhaled a deep breath for all of them. "Now."

MICHAEL ESCORTED THE TWO D.B.'s to the medical examiner's van himself while his men packed up the SWAT truck.

His team had saved nine lives today. Even the banker who'd suffered a heart attack at the beginning of the hostage crisis—when Michael had negotiated his release and begun to think that they might get through this day unscathed—

was going to pull through just fine. But it was
hard to think of this mission as a success.

Yes, the charge Delgado planted had shattered the bank's front window and ripped apart
the blinds. A split second later, Kincaid's shot
had dropped Buck like a stone.

But not before Dale Buckner had put his Smith
& Wesson to his girlfriend's heart and taken her
life with him. Not before he'd pointed his gun out
the window and fired a wild second shot.

Daphne Mullins had spent the last few hours
of her life living in terror. They'd done everything they could to save her. But in the end, it
wasn't enough. Nobody should have to live in
fear of another person like that. They should
never have to be afraid of someone who
claimed to love them. Not Daphne. Not Jillian.

Michael's fingers teased the cell phone in his
pocket as the M.E.'s van slipped away with its
police escort. He should call Jillian, make sure
she was all right. Find out if the lock had been
fixed on her apartment, if she'd had any more
disturbing contacts from Loverboy, if he'd been
on her mind even half as much this weekend as
she'd been on his.

But she was at work and he was in a mood.
No telling what raw, needy thing might come
out of his mouth right now. Besides, if he didn't

get his butt in gear and make his report to the commissioner who'd arrived on the scene, then the press would be hounding him and his men for their take on what had happened today.

KCPD commissioner Shauna Cartwright-Masterson was a far better spokesperson for the department than he could possibly be right now. His men were professionals, well trained. They'd risen to every challenge he'd put in front of them today. But it wasn't their job to handle PR right now. They needed time to themselves to work through their emotions. Taking a life was no easy thing. Losing a life was even tougher. They didn't need the media in their faces.

They all needed to blow off some steam. Holden would go home to his wife, probably go for a run with their pack of dogs and then do the things Michael remembered newlyweds doing. The other three bachelors needed to get back to headquarters, hit the showers, maybe find some friends and get something to eat or drink. Or they should go down to the Shamrock, pick up some pretty thing and get busy.

Michael needed… An image of long, coffee-colored hair and a beautiful smile flashed through his mind. Ah, hell. He tugged at the Kevlar vest he still wore, aching for some sort of release that he'd kept in check for days now. But just because he was on fire for a woman fifteen years his junior didn't mean that Jillian Masterson was feeling the same randy, needy, want-to-be-a-part-of-her-life impulses for an old warhorse like him.

"Captain Cutler?" The lady commissioner's voice cut through his thoughts, forcing him to forget about his own needs for the time being, and concentrate on making his report.

"Commissioner." Michael fell in step beside her as they moved away from the crowd to the relative privacy of the SWAT van.

"Good work, Captain."

He wasn't about to mince words. "Two people are dead, ma'am."

"Mr. Buckner?"

"Yes, ma'am."

"Any of ours?"

"No." Once she and her uniformed escort were out of sight behind the van, he turned to face her. "But the girlfriend didn't make it."

She tucked a swath of silvery blond hair behind her ear and nodded. "It could have been a lot worse, Michael. SWAT Team One secured the scene and rescued nine hostages. You kept who knows how many innocent bystanders from being hurt."

But he'd lost the girl. The commissioner could probably sense that her reassurances, while true and important to the safety of the community, hadn't tapped into his gut and eased the sense of failure he felt. Michael's gaze slid over to his men, silently stowing their gear at the back of the van. "What do I tell them to make this right?"

"This was a tough one, I know, and speculating just how much worse the result could have been if you and your men hadn't been here doesn't help right now. I'll speak to the victims' families and keep the press out of your hair. Take your men out for a drink tonight, Captain. Then go home and spend time with your son and anyone else you care about. Do something normal. Celebrate that they're safe."

Michael breathed a little easier. "Sounds like a plan."

"I understand you've been seeing my sister-in-law, Jillian."

Huh? The conversation took a sharp left and drove right into a place he wasn't ready to acknowledge yet. He propped his hand at his hip and straightened. "Jillian works with my son. I've seen her at the physical therapy clinic for several weeks now."

The commissioner's sharp eyes indicated

she knew there was more to the story than that. "Jillian can handle it if you want to talk about today."

"I'm fine."

"You're trained to listen, Michael. You're trained to keep it all inside so that there's always someone who can keep a cool head in a crisis." She reached up and patted his shoulder. "Sometimes, even the best of us have to let it out with someone we trust. Today's events might break her heart, but they wouldn't shock her. Jillian may be the baby of the family, but she's been through a lot more than you know." Probably more than Shauna knew, too, since Jillian hadn't told anyone about Loverboy's gifts and letters until he'd forced the information out of her on Friday.

"I'll be fine, ma'am," Michael reiterated.

She dropped her voice to a whisper. "Look, I promised Eli I'd keep an eye on her while he was out of town. But I won't invite her over for dinner if she has…other plans, with you."

"Don't you think I'm a little old for her? I bet her brother would."

"That card doesn't play with me, Captain. I'm ten years older than my husband." Shauna pulled back, her tone and posture dismissing him. "The heart doesn't see age when it finds what it wants."

Was Jillian what he wanted? Or did he just want to keep someone so important to his son's life safe?

Damn. He pulled back his sleeve and looked at the time. He needed to book it out of here if he wanted to get Mike over to the clinic for his afternoon session. Michael pulled out his personal phone and turned it on. "I'll be seeing her this evening. I'll give her your message."

"If you want." The commissioner laid out one last order. "Debrief at the station, but the paperwork can wait until tomorrow. Get your men out of uniform and out on the town."

"Yes, ma'am."

As the commissioner and her escort headed for the lights and microphones and waiting cameras, Michael jogged around to the back of the truck and made a quick inspection. His men were nearly ready to roll.

"Yo, Delgado." His second in command caught the helmet Michael tossed him. And while Rafe stowed it for him, Michael turned away to call Mike.

His son's cell rang and rang. What the heck? Michael tried not to remember that the last time Mike hadn't answered, he'd been lying unconscious in a mangled-up car. When it switched over to voice mail, his message was short and sweet. "It's Dad. Call me." He tried their home phone and ended up leaving a "Where are you?" on the machine there.

Michael unknowingly began to pace as he searched through his voice mail messages. Work. Work. Nothing from Mike. But there was a message from the physical therapy clinic, and another from a number he didn't recognize. He played the first.

"Michael? It's Jillian. I didn't want you to worry if you called home and no one answered. Mike's with me—has been since lunch. That clever son of a gun isn't as handicapped as he likes to claim he is. He got himself here for his therapy session. Since he was so early and there's no school to worry about, I had him stay and put him to work. You'll just need to pick him up at five when we're done." His son needed a reminder about the rule to always let him know where he was going, but Jillian's words made him smile. His go-to woman had come through for Mike again. "Oh." Her voice hushed, putting him on alert. "He sent me flowers. And a card."

Michael stopped in his tracks. The hesitant waver in her tone told him exactly which *he* she was talking about. He squeezed his eyes shut as a vivid aural memory of Daphne Mullins's sobs played in his ear. No way was he going to let that sicko Loverboy terrorize Jillian until a violent death was the only outcome left for her.

He didn't buy the false cheer in her "See you at five," nor was he waiting until the end of the day to get to her.

He smacked the driver's-side door by Rafe Delgado and signaled him to start the engine. "Let's get this show on the road."

Michael was buckled in and they were on their way to the KCPD downtown headquarters building by the time the unidentified message began to play.

"Michael?" Jillian again. He read off the number to Alex Taylor, strapped himself into the seat behind him and ordered him to track down the source. "I've got Mike at the hospital."

Everything in him tensed. *Mike?*

"Sorry, that didn't come out right. Don't worry, he's not hurt." But now Michael worried that *she* was. *Talk to me, sweetheart.* "It's, um, Troy Anthony. We were worried when he didn't show up at three, so Mike called him. Someone assaulted Troy's grandmother early this morning."

Alex Taylor interrupted. "The number's a public phone at Truman Medical Center, sir."

All eyes in the van were on their rock-still leader as the message continued. "Mike's been super with Troy—I think those two have a real bond. I'm skipping the therapy session because this is more important. We're hanging out in room 1312 at Truman Medical Center, so you can find us here when you're ready to pick him up." As proud as Michael was of his son, as hopeful as he'd been in months, there was something wrong. He heard it in the sudden hush of Jillian's voice, as if she was turning away so no one would overhear. "Michael, I… um, I think Mrs. Anthony was hurt because of me. I think *he* did it. Because she yelled at me. He told me I was welcome, as if he'd done me a favor. Maybe it's just the paint, but the things she said about her attacker… This is my fault."

No. No way.

"I saw you on the news." As if she needed something else to worry about. "Mike says that's not good. You looked tired, but okay. I hope you are. I'm so sorry about that woman. Take your time. I'll keep Mike with me as long as you need me to. Bye."

Michael saved the message. Tapped his phone against his temple. Stared at the yellow lines zipping past the center median on the road.

"Everything all right, Captain?" Delgado asked.

"Yeah." Who was he kidding? He turned to Delgado, raised his voice to be heard all the way to Trip in the back of the van. "No. I planned on taking you guys to the Shamrock tonight. Drinks on me. But you'll have to give me a rain check."

"No sweat."

"Forget it."

"We can handle it."

"Is it Mikey?"

He'd absolutely picked the best men for his team. And not just because they were each solid, skilled cops. "Mike's okay. It's a friend. Take a detour, Rafe."

The glib sergeant had already turned the van south toward the Truman Medical Center.

Chapter Seven

Jillian rubbed her hands up and down her arms, feeling a chill that went far beyond the hospital's air-conditioning, as LaKeytah Anthony repeated her story to her brother-in-law, Detective Edward Kincaid. Edward seemed skeptical that the attack on Troy's grandmother had anything to do with her, but Jillian knew. Beyond any kind of logic or circumstantial evidence, she knew.

An aunt and cousin had come to pick up Dexter to stay the night with them, but said their home was too small to accommodate Troy's wheelchair. Troy had covered the slight by insisting he wanted to stay at his grandmother's side. He claimed he was old enough and independent enough to stay on his own.

At sixteen? In the same building where LaKeytah had been given a concussion, along with a broken arm and jaw? Nobody should be alone when his family had come under attack like that.

But her compassion for Troy didn't make it any easier to stand here in the dimly lit room and listen to LaKeytah Anthony's story.

With LaKeytah's jaw wired shut and her body sedated to ease the pain, her words slurred and her eyes kept drifting out of focus. But the older woman seemed perfectly clear on the details. "He hit me from behind. And then I don't know much of anything. I never saw his face—only know it was a man by the pitch of his voice. He said it was a warning, that the world was an ugly place for a lot of people, and that I didn't have the right to take out my anger and frustration on anyone else and add to their burden."

Which was exactly what she'd done to Jillian the evening she'd gotten Troy home late.

"He said…" a tear leaked from beneath LaKeytah's closed eyelid, and Jillian nearly wept with her "…there would be no second chance…to keep my mouth shut."

Jillian shivered in the doorway and suddenly felt a hand nudging hers away from her arm and giving it a squeeze.

Mike's young face was creased with concern. "You okay?"

No, she wasn't. She squeezed back and smiled. "Will you stay with Troy? I don't think he should be alone right now. I need to get some fresh air."

He nodded and Jillian slipped into the hallway. She leaned back against the wall just outside the door and shuddered with a weary, wary breath. Was this her fault? Did Loverboy think this was what she wanted? Was this his twisted way of taking care of her? And how did he know LaKeytah Anthony had reamed her out in the first place?

Did he live in Troy's building? His neighborhood? Isaac Rush and Mr. Lynch instantly came to mind. She knew Isaac to be violent, but dishing out vigilante justice if there was no profit to be made? And Mr. Lynch was certainly big enough and powerful enough to have carried out the attack LaKeytah described. But what was his motive? If defending her truly was the reason for the assault, it made no sense. They'd only ever really talked that one night. The night he'd pulled her out of Isaac's bed and sent her to the police station to file charges of attempted rape. No. He had nothing to do with her life.

So did that mean Loverboy had followed her to Troy's building? Was his attention about more than letters and flowers? Her skin crawled at the notion that he could be watching her, even now. "Oh, God."

Jillian swept the hallway with her gaze. Was that him? The orderly with the cart? The bleary-eyed intern? She thought she was going to be sick.

Needing something, anything, to do besides stand here and suspect every man she saw—doctor, visitor, patient—she spotted the water fountain near the floor's main desk and made a beeline for it. She splashed a palmful of cool water on her cheeks and neck and then leaned over to get a drink.

A hand brushed her shoulder. "Jilly? What are you doing here?"

"Don't touch—" The solicitous voice startled her and she spun around, spraying the man in the white lab coat with the water drops that clung to her hair. "Dr. Randolph." She pressed her fingers to her lips, embarrassed to wear her fears so close to the surface and have greeted an old friend so rudely. "Sorry. I didn't realize it was you."

Bushy brows that matched his short, silvering hair arched behind his glasses. "Are you all right? Is someone in your family hurt?"

"Oh, no. No, no. Holly and her husband, Eli and his wife, they're all fine."

"I'm relieved to hear that." He hunched his lanky shoulders and looked straight into her eyes. "You're not…?"

She knew that look—had hated it when she'd been seventeen and sitting through her first group therapy sessions at the Boatman Rehabilitation Clinic. There was something strengthening about being able to dismiss his concern. "I'm not looking for a meeting." Reaching into her pocket, Jillian pulled out her keys and dangled her ten-year sobriety key fob for him to see. "I'm still being good."

A kind eye winked as he straightened. "Glad to hear it."

She shouldn't have been surprised to run into Wayne Randolph at the medical center. Though she knew him from rehab and private counseling sessions over the years since, Dr. Randolph also practiced psychology at the hospital, assessing patients and directing them into various mental health programs that complemented the physical care the medical staff provided.

He put those assessing skills to good use. "You never answered my question. Why are you here?"

She linked her hand through his arm and walked him a few steps away from the fountain to give the next person in line the chance to get a drink without eavesdropping on their conversation. "The guardian of one of my patients was assaulted."

"Was she hurt badly?"

"Badly enough to be hospitalized for a few days. A lot of weird things have been happening lately. This is the worst of it so far."

"So far?" He rested his hand over hers on his arm and gave it a fatherly pat. "My goodness, dear. Are you in trouble? Can I help? Do you need to talk?"

"Always the therapist, aren't you?" Jillian shook her head. "You know, sometimes I think…"

"What?"

Why not? Dr. Randolph would understand this more than anyone she knew. "Do you think horrible things like this happen around me because of the destructive choices I used to make back in high school? Are other people paying for my mistakes?"

"You mean like cosmic retribution for a misspent youth?" Dr. Randolph turned her in his arms and pulled her in for a hug. "No. Sometimes, bad things just happen." He patted her hair and rocked her like a little girl. "You were one of the strongest young women I ever worked with, Jilly. I always knew you would turn your life around. And now you've gone on to do good things for so many other people. If anything, you've learned from your mistakes, and are making the world a better place because of it."

Trading one last hug around his waist, Jillian pulled away, appreciating the kind words if not fully believing them. "It is good to see a friendly face, Doc. I'd better get back to my friends. See if I can help."

"All right. Remember to call my office for an appointment if you decide you need to talk about anything."

"I will. Thanks."

Feeling marginally better, and slightly less paranoid, she headed back to LaKeytah Anthony's room. A nurse went in before Jillian could reach it and shooed out all her visitors. Troy came out first, looking more subdued than she'd ever seen him. Mike wheeled his chair out behind him.

"Maybe I'm not good for anything anymore," Troy muttered, as if repeating words he'd just heard. Jillian's heart twisted in her chest. "I can't blame her for puttin' her heart and soul into Dexter now."

"She's doped up on pain meds, man." Mike nudged his friend in the arm. "You remember what that was like. She doesn't know what she's saying. She didn't mean it."

"I should have done something," Troy insisted. "I'm the man of the house." Displaying a rare burst of temper, Troy smacked the arm of his chair. "If I wasn't in this damn wheelchair…"

Mike didn't have a good answer for that one and looked equally dejected. Jillian hastened her steps, intending to intervene, but Mike came up with an alternate strategy of his own. "Hey, dude, you hungry?"

Troy shrugged. "Whatever."

"I know a shortcut to the cafeteria."

"Okay."

As the two teens rolled around the corner, Jillian shook her head, marveling at the resiliency of youth. Underneath all that attitude, Mike Cutler was a natural. Compassionate. Intuitive. He had so much to offer the world if he'd give himself half a chance.

Edward came out of the room next, softly closing the door behind him. He draped an arm around her shoulders. "I've gotten all I can get from Mrs. Anthony right now. The nurse says she needs her rest."

"What I said makes sense, right? I feel like I should apologize to her."

"You'll do no such thing." Edward's tone was adamant. "I get the idea from Troy that his grandmother yells a lot. There's no evidence to prove you had anything to do with the motive for her attack, beyond freaky coincidence. I've got my notes and the card from the flowers you gave me to add to your file, and I'll keep in touch with the detective assigned to Mrs. Anthony's case. But right now, unless the lab comes up with something concrete to tie it all together, we just have to sit and wait and keep a close eye on you." He hugged her close and pressed a kiss to temple. "Love you, kiddo. Call if you need anything."

"I will." Jillian shivered when he released her and automatically hugged her arms around her middle.

The scar on his jaw throbbed with concern. "You gonna be okay?"

"As long as that whack job is out there terrorizing me and hurting others in the name of love?" She shook her head. "I don't think I'm ever going to feel okay."

"I do." Edward was looking over her shoulder. "Turn around."

Frowning at the odd request, Jillian turned. Her breath caught in her chest, then rushed out in easier, quicker gasps.

Michael Cutler was striding down the hallway. Tall, intent, black hair rumpled.

Wearing his uniform and needing a shave. Walking straight toward her.

"See ya, kiddo."

Jillian barely heard Edward's goodbye. She was already rushing forward, her eyes locked on to the mesmerizing strength of midnight blue. "Michael? Are you all right?"

She didn't pause, she didn't ask—she zoomed right up to Michael, locked her arms around his waist and turned her ear to his starched shirt and the strong beat of his heart underneath.

He braced his feet to catch her and wrapped his arms around her, burying his nose against her hair. "I'm okay. Are you safe?"

"But the news about the hostages at the bank, I saw—"

"Damn it, woman, I'm worried about *you.*" He leaned back, caught her face between his hands. He smoothed her hair off her cheek and tucked the loose strands behind her ears. He read every nuance of her upturned eyes, every catch or gasp of breath. He brushed the rough pads of his fingers across her brows, her cheeks, her jaw, her mouth. He pressed his thumb against the swell of her bottom lip and went still. "I don't scare easily, sweetheart, but your messages…"

"I'm okay." Her whispered words transformed the touch of his fingers into a caress against her lips. "Better, now that you're here. But I'm okay."

Instead of giving a verbal response to her mushy confession, his gaze darted to the right and the left. Then he grabbed her by the hand and led her down the hall to an empty patient room. "Is Mike around?"

He pulled her inside. "He took Troy to the cafeteria to eat."

"Neither one's hurt? Upset?" The door closed.

"A little shaken, but they'll be fine." He took her by the shoulders and pushed her back against the wall beside the door. "Michael?"

He kissed her.

An almost angry stamp on her lips at first. And then he cupped her face and angled her mouth and covered her mouth in a kiss that was as gentle as it was hungry, as thorough as it was needy. Winding her fingers into the collar of his shirt, Jillian parted her lips and kissed him back.

She quickly realized it was pent-up desire and fear and confusion and want, not anger that made the kiss so powerful, so crazy. Because Jillian was feeling it, too.

The tension between them had simmered for

months, excused as latent attraction to a handsome, healthy man. She rose on tiptoe and wound her arms around Michael's neck, her palms tingling at the contrast between his starchy uniform and his short, silky hair.

The fears she felt—for her own safety, for his—had brought that tension to the surface, made it harder and harder to filter her feelings through polite decorum. He had a hang-up about their difference in ages; they both wanted to put his son before whatever it was they were feeling.

Michael's tongue slid between her lips and rubbed against hers, creating friction and heat and the desire to conduct her own exploration. She stroked smooth, firm lips, delighted at the rasp of beard stubble against her softer skin, tasted coffee on his tongue. Oh, yeah. They were way more than *just friends*.

He pulled her away from the wall into the hardness of his chest. His hand slid down her back to squeeze her bottom and lift right into the swelling evidence of his desire for her. Jillian moaned as her body absorbed and reacted to sensation after sensation. Her small breasts felt tight and womanly, rubbing against him. Her lips felt swollen, feverish, sexy. Her heart pounded against her ribs and she felt hot, heavy, farther down.

"Michael…" She peppered kisses along his neck, his jaw, his chin—anything he'd let her reach as he turned his attentions to the rapid pulse beating along the side of her neck.

It was an emotional release, a catharsis for them both.

"So pretty. So strong. So hot. So good. I need…" He breathed against her ear. His arms tightened around her, shook.

"What do you need, Michael? Please tell me what you need."

He pulled the band from her hair, sifted his fingers through its length, buried his nose in a handful of it and breathed deeply. "God, I need…"

At this moment, in this room, she'd give him whatever he wanted.

Instead, Jillian's toes touched the floor. Then she was standing flat-footed. And then she was leaning back against the wall for support, panting as Michael scrubbed his palm over his face and backed away.

Breathing just as hard, he shot his fingers through his short, ruffed hair and held out his hand, as though warding away temptation itself. "This can't happen. This shouldn't happen."

"Why? If I want it, too?" She pushed away from the wall.

He retreated a step. "I won't take advantage of your vulnerable state just because I had a lousy day and I'm freaking out of control!"

She'd never heard him raise his voice before, and though the force of it stung, she suspected it wasn't directed at her. His shoulders lifted with a deep breath and heartbeat by heartbeat, she saw the invisible armor of his captain's uniform slide back into place. "I'll get it together. I promise." He paced across the room and came back a different man than the passionate, open one who had nearly seduced her a moment ago. "Explain the situation to me. Tell me what we need to do."

Angered that he was taking the blame for what had happened, hurt that he thought she wasn't old enough or sensible enough or experienced enough to know her own desires, Jillian retrieved the rubber band from beneath the nearest bed and tugged her hair back into a messy ponytail. "For one thing, don't be so hard on yourself. It took the two of us to make that kiss happen."

"I'm talking about the messages, the attack on Mrs. Anthony. I'm talking about Troy and Mike and their welfare."

"I know what you're talking about." She was raw and achy and mad as hell that he refused to acknowledge the connection between them. "You're talking about being a cop. You're talking about being a father. But I don't think you're comfortable talking about being a man. Not one who feels things and wants things. Not one who might need something for himself. At least, not around me."

A pulse beat in the tight clench of his chiseled jaw, as he threw every bit of his considerable authority into the stiffness of his posture. But the steeliness wavered in his dark blue eyes and Jillian's anger immediately dissipated.

"I'm sorry. That wasn't fair to say. I know we each have a lot on our plates right now, things that take priority over…a relationship."

He braced his hands at his hips, relaxing a fraction. "So you see why a…relationship… shouldn't happen between us?"

"No." She pressed her hand to his chest to silence his argument. "But I see why it shouldn't happen right now."

She turned and pulled open the door.

"Jillian…"

"Troy needs a place to stay," she stated without looking back. "I'd take him home with me but I don't know if the clinic would think that was appropriate. Besides…" She felt Michael's heat, coming up behind her. She saw his hand on the door above hers. "I don't know if it would be safe for him there."

"Troy has a place to stay. He'll come home with Mike and me. The house is completely handicap-accessible. It would probably do them both some good to spend more time together."

Finally, Jillian turned to face him. "You'll take Troy in?"

"If he accepts the invitation."

"Thank you." Couldn't he see what a great team they made? How could Michael deny this bond between them? Maybe he just wanted to deny he'd discovered it with *her.* A recovering addict with a stalker in pursuit probably wouldn't be any man's first choice for a mate, no matter what attraction sizzled between them. And she was especially unsuitable for a man of Michael's responsibilities and reputation. Acceptance had always been a big part of moving on with her life. "We're still friends, right?"

After a moment, Michael nodded. "Friends."

Despite the iron fist of reality crushing her heart, Jillian stretched up to press a kiss to his jaw. "Thank you."

Chapter Eight

Anyone Jillian might want to see on the street in front of Troy's apartment building was smart enough to be safely locked up inside their homes at this time of night. Chattering girls. Decent working folk. Shopkeepers trying to make an honest profit. There wasn't a one of them in sight as Michael steered his extended-cab pickup into a parking place across the street.

Instead, there were hookers and junkies and other souls that she'd just as soon would stay in the shadows where they lurked. Even the trio of homeless men hanging back in the alley, standing around the trash can fire they'd built, knew enough to stay off the streets of No-Man's Land after dark.

Michael shifted the truck into Park and left the engine idling as he scanned the sidewalks and parked cars around them. Jillian clutched the dashboard, her own trepidation growing as he leaned against the window and looked up at the apartments across the street. She knew he was seeing and evaluating every potential danger.

"I see a lot of lights on the fifth floor," Michael observed. "That means the neighbors are still up. Yours is the one on the end, right, Troy?"

"Yes, sir."

Michael had taken the time at the police station to change into his civvies when she'd driven him over from the hospital to pick up his truck. But he still wore his gun and badge in plain view on his belt. He was expecting trouble, and because Michael did, Jillian expected it, too.

He braced his arm on the back of the seat and turned to the teenage boys seated behind them. "You ready? We'll go up to your apartment, pack whatever you need and get on the road to our house ASAP. All right?"

Even though this was the place Troy called home, she could see he wasn't particularly comforted about being here. "If it's all the same to you, Mr. Cutler, I'd rather not go in. I don't know if the super's got Grandma's blood cleaned out of the elevator yet." Jillian's breath stuttered right along with his at the sickening image. "I don't think I can go in there again if he hasn't. Here are the keys."

Michael took the keys and closed them in his fist. "All right. I'll go." He looked across the front seat to Jillian. "I want you to slide over here behind the wheel. Be ready to drive off if anybody who shouldn't approaches the truck."

"It'll be quicker if I do it," Jillian suggested. "I've been in the apartment before and know where things are. Then we can all get out of here sooner."

"I'm not letting you go in there by yourself. That was the whole point of me driving."

"You're not coming with me and leaving these boys alone here." Jillian reached for the door handle. "I'll go."

"I'd rather call for backup."

"And wait even longer? These boys shouldn't be here."

"*You* shouldn't be here," he insisted. He slipped his hand across the seat until it rested next to hers. "Jillian, is this about what happened at the hospital? Are we going to fight about everything now?"

"What happened at the hospital?" Mike asked from the backseat.

"Nothing." They answered in unison, showing the boys that there was a new kind of tension simmering between the adults in the front seat.

Jillian took a stab at offering an honest explanation. "We had a disagreement about…how to proceed with—"

"Events that have happened today," Michael finished, discreetly leaving out any mention of kisses and confessions and decisions that a relationship with Michael Cutler was out of the question.

"I just asked." Mike crossed his arms and sank back into his seat.

"Son, I'm sorry. I've got a lot on my mind right now. I'll try to explain it better later."

"Whatever."

With the air inside the truck thick enough to slice, someone needed to break the tension. Jillian volunteered. She moved her left hand to let her fingers slide over Michael's. "I'm picking up clothes, a toothbrush and Troy's meds. Once I'm inside the lobby, the doors will lock behind me and the security light will come on. Right, Troy?"

"Yeah."

Michael spread his fingers to capture hers between them. "Mrs. Anthony was attacked in the lobby," he pointed out.

"Fine. If I see or hear anything suspicious, I'll come right back out. When I get into the apartment, I'll turn the light on so you'll know

I'm there. I'll turn it off when I leave. I'll lock
every door as soon as I'm through it." She was
trying to come up with a reasonable plan. "Give
me ten minutes—fifteen tops. If I'm not back,
you lock these boys in and come get me."

He turned their hands, pressing the keys into
her palm and curling her fingers around them.
"I'll give you ten."

Jillian felt three sets of eyes on her every
step of the way across the street and into the
building. When she was secured inside the glass
double doors, the light came on and she turned
and waved to show she was safe. Michael
answered by pointing his finger and insisting
she get a move on.

Keeping her eyes and ears tuned to any sign
of movement, she pushed the elevator button
and waited as its gears churned into action.
Hopefully, if others had been using the elevator,
that meant Troy's fears had been unfounded
and the elevator had been cleaned of all signs
of the attack.

But waiting meant she had time on her
hands—only seconds, perhaps, but time
enough to think. Time enough to *feel* every
detail around her and take notice of the subtle
warnings she should be paying attention to. The
super's light kept the lobby brightly lit, but

made it difficult to see down the first-floor hallway. And from this angle, the light reflected off the glass doors, creating a visual barrier between her and the reassuring sight of the black pickup parked across the street.

Jillian tucked her ponytail inside her jacket and zipped it up to the collar of her polo. No sense giving a perp something easy to grab on to. Just where had LaKeytah's attacker been hiding? In that corner? In that one? She arranged the fleece-lined hood around her neck, easing the prickle of awareness that raised the delicate hairs along her nape. The elevator dinged on a floor above her, meaning it had stopped for someone else to get in. Did she want to wait to see who might walk out, or worse, who might decide to share a ride back up with her?

Pulling her cell phone from her pocket, Jillian scrolled through her numbers until she found Michael's. She centered it on the screen and rested her thumb on Send in case she needed to speed-dial him for help. One by one, she slipped Troy's keys between the fingers of her right hand, giving herself at least some kind of weapon to defend herself with if necessary.

The longer she waited, the more her thoughts took hold.

She couldn't smell the ammonia odor from the apartment with all the cats, but she could detect the hint of something else in the air. A hint of musk, like men's cologne. The scent seemed familiar but Jillian couldn't place it. And delicate as it was, as though the man wearing the cologne had walked through the lobby some time ago, or was standing at a great distance, the air around her suddenly grew cloying.

As if the scent was closing in on her.

As if the man who belonged to that scent was closing in.

Who was she kidding? She was done waiting here.

Five flights of stairs was an easy climb for a woman who ran wind sprints or jogged nearly every day of her life. The concrete and steel stairs had a light on each landing and were blessedly devoid of company and perfumey smells. The physical exertion also worked some magic at toning down her paranoia. *Just keep moving. Don't think.* Jillian was barely breathing hard by the time she reached the fifth floor and opened the service door. She quickly got inside the Anthonys' apartment and locked the door behind her.

Light on. Grab gym bag from Troy's closet. Pack clothes, pack underwear. Pack iPod and ear buds—no teen should be without his music. Move to bathroom for toothbrush, into kitchen for pill bottles in cabinet. Snatch family photo off refrigerator and stuff into bag. Zip it shut. Check time. Smile. She'd make ten minutes with time to spare. Light off. Lock door.

Jillian didn't even bother with the elevator. Slinging the bag over her shoulder, she headed straight for the stairs. But the descent didn't go quickly or smoothly.

She had her foot on the first step off the fourth-floor landing when she smelled it and stopped. She sniffed the air. Not that sick cologne scent. Something acrid. Chemical.

Something burning.

Clutching the railing, she moved down several steps, bringing herself closer to identifying the sour stench. She stopped again. Not a fire, but something long forgotten and all too familiar.

Someone in the stairwell was smoking crack.

"Oh, jeez," she whispered as a shiver rippled down her spine. It wasn't temptation she was feeling, but shame. She squeezed her eyes shut against a flashback of familiarity. Crack might not have been her drug of choice, but this had once been her world. Hiding out in empty stairwells and abandoned rooms, escaping reality, losing herself. Why had she ever let herself become a part of this?

How could she ever really leave it behind and be the strong, worthy, loving—loved— woman she fought every day to be when this was still so very real for her?

"Stop it." Jillian tried to shake the thoughts out of her head. Those were just the kind of debilitating mind games Dr. Randolph had worked so hard with her on to overcome. Under his guidance, she'd learned how to turn her experience into knowledge that could help others. She'd learned to use her talents as therapy, and turn her weaknesses into strength. She could overcome grief, she could over- come drugs, she could overcome anything— just as long as *she* believed she could do it. She'd kicked her addiction. She'd gotten healthy. She was making a difference in the world now.

She could damn well pack a bag and get back down these stairs.

At the third-floor landing, she was close enough to hear the voices.

"I never thought I'd see this day, Rivers."

Rivers? Blake?

Jillian inched around the corner, her heart crying with concern for a friend who hadn't been able to find his way out of the past the way she had.

"Hey!" She jerked back at the sound of a thud and a grunt, hating that she recognized Blake's slurred southern drawl. "I wasn't dealin', man. We were sharing. I wouldn't step on your turf, Isaac. You know I wouldn't do that."

Her own stomach muscles clenched at the next thud and breathless curse. She reached into her pocket for her phone. And Michael.

"Then where'd you get the money?" Isaac Rush's voice was crystal clear.

"It's mine. I earned it."

"Selling this? She's *my* customer."

Thud.

Blake gasped for breath. "Hell, man. I've got money. I buy from you. You know I've always been good—" Another punch. A fit of coughing.

Jillian felt every blow with him.

"You can't sell what I give you without giving me a cut of the profit. You understand?" A moment of silence. Footsteps heading down the stairs. "I don't think he does."

"That's my cash!" Blake protested.

And then the beat-down started in earnest.

Jillian pressed Send and ran down the stairs. "Stop it. Stop it!"

She stepped over the pipe and the passed-out woman on the stairs and rounded the corner in time to see Mr. Lynch throw Blake up against the wall of the second-floor landing. The black man's coat swung around him like a cape as he pulled his gloved fist back to strike another blow. Blake put up his hands and staggered, begging for mercy. But with his puffy eye and bleeding lip, Jillian didn't wait to see if he'd crumple to the floor or suffer another punch.

"Stop!" She dropped the bag and ran straight down to Blake, putting herself between him and Lynch.

"Mr. Rush?" Lynch's dark eyes fixed on her upturned face as he called down to his boss. For a split second, his big fist hovered in the air, but he stayed his hand. He pulled back the front of his coat, needlessly reminding her of the gun he carried. "Don't do this, girl," he warned. "Get out of the way."

Blake's clumsy hands clamped down on Jillian's shoulders and her knees nearly buckled as he leaned his weight against her in an effort to stay on his feet. "I traded tit for tat with her. I didn't do anything wrong," he spat beside Jillian's ear.

"That's not how Mr. Rush sees it."

"He sees what he wants. Takes what he wants."

"Blake, shut up." She turned and slid beneath his arm, propping him up as she tugged at his waist. "Let's just go."

"Jilly." Isaac Rush turned the corner, blocking their slim escape route around Lynch's broad shoulders. "You decided to take me up on my offer, after all."

"No." When he reached for her hand, Jillian jumped back, knocking Blake back into the wall, accidentally jabbing her elbow into his ribs. "I'm helping out a friend. We just want to leave."

Blake cursed, too blinded by pain and the drug in his system to understand the danger they faced. "You tell him, baby."

Isaac sneered. "Is this what you ended up with, sugar? A man who pays to get laid? I was first class with you all the way. I can hook you up with something good, I promise. Nothing cut-rate like Loverboy here."

Loverboy?

The unfortunate choice of words pierced the bubble of adrenaline that had sent her charging down these stairs and fueled her defiance. Now she could see the folly of trying to rescue anyone.

Out of bravado, but not out of hope, she turned a pleading eye up to Mr. Lynch. "Let us go. Please. The same way you let me go that night. I know you remember."

The hand on the gun never wavered. "I remember."

"What's she talking about, Lynch?" Isaac didn't sound pleased.

"You don't belong here, girl."

"Neither does he. Please let us go." She thought she detected a subtle shift in Lynch's position, screening Isaac from direct view. Jillian didn't wait for a better opportunity to escape. She tugged. "Come with me, Blake."

But the idiot still had enough ego in him to keep his mouth going. "You've gone soft, Lynch. You're not so tough against both of us, are you?"

Lynch made a growling sound and lunged at Blake.

Blake yanked Jillian in front of him like a shield. Their feet tangled and Blake fell, pulling her with him.

Glass shattered. Men shouted. Someone cursed.

"Jillian!"

She heard her name, but her chin clipped the railing, and her skull rang with the impact, distorting the voices around her. Blake came down on top of her and her knee cracked against a step, shooting pain all the way down to her toes. She curled into a ball as much as she could and tumbled down to the next landing where she landed with a jolt on top of Blake.

"Jillian!"

"KCPD. On the ground. Now."

"Back off!"

"Easy, pal. Don't move."

"I'll take that."

Hands were on her, pulling her off Blake's chest, lifting her from harm's way. Her head throbbed. Her leg ached. Every movement seemed to reveal another bruise.

"Careful," a deep voice snapped beside her ear. "Cover him."

"He's clean, boss."

Twin steel bands caught her behind her back and legs, and her cheek lolled against solid, encompassing warmth. The pure, clean scent of soap filled her nose and nubby wool tickled her skin. She was sinking into a cozy heat until a jolt of pressure stabbed her chin. "Ow!"

Her eyes blinked open. Her foggy brain began to clear.

"Jillian?" Long, sure fingers were unzipping her jacket. "I need your sweatshirt, okay, sweetheart?"

She nodded, trusting the voice if not fully comprehending the words. Jillian sat up and lifted her arms when requested. The long fingers were red and wet with blood. She looked down and watched it drip onto her polo shirt. Her blood. "Oh. Did I…?"

"Are you hurt anywhere else? Twist anything?"

"I bumped my knee."

A firm hand probed her leg and she winced when it found the swelling around her kneecap.

"Nothing broken."

"She okay, boss?"

The last of the fog drifted away and Jillian realized she was sitting in Michael Cutler's lap at the bottom of the stairs. She was hurt, but he was here, pressing her wadded-up jacket against her chin to stanch her wound. She was safe. With him around, she would always be safe. "Michael?"

Dark blue eyes locked on to hers, searching for something. And then he nodded. "She'll be okay. Delgado?"

"This one's out cold. But he's still breathing."

"Taylor?"

"The girl's coming around, but she's pretty mellow."

Delgado? Taylor? She knew those names. Jillian lifted her gaze to follow the angle of Michael's commands.

The stairwell was swarming with cops— three of them, at any rate. Alex Taylor came from upstairs, his badge hanging from a chain around his neck over the football jersey he wore. He guided the blank-eyed hooker onto the step beside Isaac Rush, who sat glaring into space, his hands bound together by his own necktie. Michael tossed a pair of handcuffs to the blond she recognized as Holden Kincaid in the lobby. He wore his badge clipped to the front pocket of his jeans and a gun tucked into the back of his belt. A second gun he held in his hand never moved away from the supine form of Mr. Lynch, even as he locked the cuffs around the black man's wrists. A third cop, Rafe Delgado, with blue-black hair and olive skin, knelt over Blake's body on the landing above her.

Blake's body? Jillian jerked in Michael's lap, trying to scramble to her feet.

"Easy," Michael warned, looping his arm around her waist and anchoring her into place.

"Is he…?"

"He's alive, ma'am," Delgado answered. "But we need to get him to a hospital."

"Lucky bastard," Isaac whined. "He was willing to sacrifice Jilly to get out of here in one piece."

"Enough." The short cop in the football jersey pulled his gun and urged Isaac to be silent.

"Holster that, Taylor," Michael ordered. "These are too tight quarters and somebody might get hurt."

"Yeah, Taylor," Isaac mimicked, "put that gun away before you hurt the boss's lady."

Jillian felt the tension that stiffened Michael's body, but his steady gaze never blinked as it shifted to Isaac. "Put a muzzle on it."

Isaac shrugged. "Hey, we were trying to keep the lady safe, too. Jilly and I are old friends. Mr. Lynch and I were trying to convince her to leave when Rivers there went nutso on us."

Old friends? The gulf between Michael and Jillian widened. It didn't matter what she felt for him—that she was falling in love with him. A veteran cop who commanded men like these and a former teen addict who'd run the streets and spent time with the likes of Isaac Rush? Yeah. That was a relationship that was gonna happen. Try introducing her as Mike's stepmom or taking her to a dinner with his departmental colleagues. Whatever Michael felt for her, he didn't *want* to feel. He was just a good cop. A good man. Doing the right thing. He'd protect her. He'd be her friend.

But love her?

Maybe her heart should set its sights a little

lower. Maybe she should focus on her work and her patients and forget about a happily-ever-after with this man.

Suddenly, the shelter of Michael's body felt like a trap, one she was embarrassed to be caught in. Jillian pushed against the arm at her waist and struggled to get to her feet.

Instead of freeing herself, she wound up clinging to Michael's shoulders as he shifted his hold on her and stood with her in his arms. "Rafe, you have things under control here?"

"Yes, sir. Bus is en route for this guy. Perps are secure."

"Good. Wait for the local boys to get here and make the arrests. I don't want to step on anybody's toes. I'm taking Jillian out to my truck."

"Put me down." Jillian flattened her palm against his chest and tried to push away. "It's just some bruises and a cut on my chin. I can walk."

"Humor me." He strode across the lobby, his boots crunching over shattered glass from around the door lock. "Seems the only way I can know you're safe is to hold on to you."

"I was only trying to help."

"Just keep that cloth on the wound. I think you'll need stitches."

Resigning herself to the humiliation of

causing this man more trouble than she was worth, Jillian dutifully wound her arm around his neck and wedged her jacket beneath her chin. "Kincaid," he snapped. "Get the doors and take that bag out to my truck. I'm driving her to the E.R. myself."

"Yes, sir."

The few curiosity-seekers who'd gathered to see what the crookedly parked vehicles and flashing red and white lights were all about moved in to get a closer look at the tall man with the black-and-silver hair carrying the injured woman with the pale resignation on her face across the street. They cleared a path for him, and scattered entirely when a man built like a tank got out of the cab of Michael's truck and circled around to open the passenger-side door. Another cop?

Michael finally set her down on the passenger seat and secured her safety belt over her lap. "Thanks, Trip." He dismissed the off-duty officer who'd stayed outside to protect Troy and Mike. "Better get across the street and keep these people from contaminating the scene until backup gets here."

"Yes, sir." He tipped the brim of the KCPD ball cap he wore. "Ma'am."

As soon as Michael closed the door and

opened a bin in the back of his truck to secure the bag and pull out something else, Mike and Troy scooted forward.

"Jillian?"

"You okay?"

With the combination of blood and being carried out, the boys were understandably concerned.

She reached over the back of the seat to squeeze their hands. "Cuts on the head and face bleed a lot because the blood vessels are so close to the surface. It probably looks worse than it is."

"It looks sick to me." Troy pointed to her chin. The driver's door opened and Michael climbed in. "Did that guy attack you? Did you see his face? Did the cops arrest him?"

"The police have everything under control, Troy," Michael stated, turning the key in the ignition. "We're all safe." Except maybe Jillian, judging by the death ray of don't-you-ever-scare-me-like-that-again shining from his eyes. "Everybody buckle up. Here."

He reached across her to pull a first-aid kit from the glove compartment. With swift, sure fingers that were still marked by her blood, he unwrapped a wad of gauze and ripped open some adhesive tape. He tossed her ruined jacket to the floor at her feet and replaced it with a more sanitary wrap.

His movements were precise, yet gentle, as he shook out his black insulated KCPD jacket and tucked it around her like a blanket. "Don't you go into shock on me." He tapped the crude bandage on her chin. "Keep the pressure on that."

Mike reached over the seat and rested a hand on Jillian's shoulder. "I'll make sure she does."

Touched by the maturity of his concern for her, Jillian covered his hand with hers and held on.

Michael flashed his lights, honked his horn and pulled out. With some hard turns, he wove his way through the parked vehicles his team had left in the middle of the street and stepped on the accelerator.

"Did I get hit on the head, or did the cavalry just come to my rescue?"

Mike squeezed her shoulder. "Dad called his team as soon as you left the truck."

Michael slowed to take a corner. "Fortunately, they were all in one place. The Shamrock's not that far away."

"The Shamrock Bar?" Jillian asked.

"You know it?"

"A lot of the PTs and hospital staff go there for happy hour."

"A lot of cops do, too."

They fell into a long, awkward silence as Michael sped through lights and zipped through downtown Kansas City to get her to the Truman Medical Center.

The bright lights marking the emergency room's canopied entrance were in sight when she spoke again. "I was just trying to help a friend."

"I know. You're always out to save somebody, no matter what the risk is to yourself." He pulled into the parking lot and found a space close to the entrance. After he shut off the engine, he turned to her. "Did you ever consider that maybe one of those *friends* is particularly grateful for what you've done for them?"

"You mean the letters?" She patted the air, silently asking him to drop the subject in front of the boys.

"What letters?" Troy asked.

But Captain Cutler was nothing if not thorough. "I mean the letters, the flowers, the watching, the favors you don't want, the making you afraid."

"A friend wouldn't do that to me."

"A friend wouldn't use you as a shield in the middle of a fight, either."

"Blake didn't…he wouldn't."

"He did." He pulled his phone from his belt and held it up in his fist. "I heard every damn word."

"Dad!" The crackle of worry in Mike's voice shushed the debate. "Scaring Jillian won't help right now. You didn't lose her. We…didn't lose her. Just get her inside and make sure she's okay."

Michael's face betrayed pain when he looked back at his son. Then he scrubbed his hand over his jaw, taking the emotions with it. "Smart kid." He reached back and cupped Mike's cheek. "Damn smart kid. I guess I'm the one who's scared."

He gave Mike a fatherly pat and then got out. When he opened Jillian's door, she'd turned to climb down, but Michael blocked her path. He cupped her face in the same tender gesture he'd used on his son, only there was no good-ol'-boy pat on the cheek. "You've touched a lot of lives, Jillian—ours included. I think you *know* the man who is sending you those letters. He's around you somewhere in your life, a lot closer than you might think. He doesn't care about the good you put into the world. That's what scares me."

And then he kissed her. In front of his son, in front of Troy, in front of the waiting E.R. attendant with a wheelchair. No subtle touch, no secret room. He kissed her softly, gently, thoroughly. Jillian snuggled inside the heat and scent of Michael's jacket around her and leaned into the kiss. His lips cherished hers, his calloused fingers soothed her feverish skin. Inside, she was melting, wanting, weeping at the poignancy of his tender kiss.

There was no more falling in love with this man. She was there. She wasn't sure how the two of them together could ever work beyond moments like this, but there was no doubt in her heart that she loved him.

Perhaps succumbing to the "whoa" and "Go, Captain" and nervous laughs from the backseat, Michael broke off the kiss with an aching sigh, picked her up and set her down in the waiting wheelchair himself.

But out of earshot of the boys, he had one more sobering warning to whisper against her hair as he pushed her inside the hospital. And a promise. "Tonight we were lucky. My men were close by. But I'm not going to trust that will happen the next time. When I take Troy home with us tonight, you're coming, too."

Chapter Nine

"I'd have bet good money that two sixteen-year-olds with pizza, pop and no school to worry about would have been pulling an all-nighter." Michael opened the door to what had once been Mike's bedroom before the leg braces and wheelchair had forced him to move down to the first floor. He raised his voice so that Jillian could still hear him in the bathroom across the hall as he tossed a set of sheets onto the bare mattress and started making up the bed. "Mike and Troy are both zonked out downstairs. I turned off the game they were playing and covered them up."

"It's awfully late, even for night owls."

Michael turned at the breathy voice in the doorway behind him—in time to catch Jillian in the middle of a yawn that stretched her freshly washed face. After a couple of hours in the E.R., getting stitches in her chin and an

X-ray of her knee to ensure that nothing was broken, the hot shower had gone a long way to wash away the memory of seeing her dazed and bleeding at the bottom of a stairwell with an armed Goliath, a known drug dealer and that weasel of an ex-boyfriend all trying to get their paws on her.

Now he wished he'd thought to offer her some fresh clothes to replace the ones she'd put back on. Her sweatshirt jacket and royal-blue polo had been stained with blood and grime, and disposed of at the hospital. That left her in a white tank top and her torn khaki pants—and the black KCPD jacket she'd adopted since he'd covered her with it in No-Man's Land. With the insulated sleeves rolled above her wrists and the collar turned up around her neck, it seemed as though she'd turned his working jacket into a robe.

The shoulders were too big for her, and her slim, athletic frame swam inside the girth of it. But he decided he liked the way it looked on her. It was probably some male instinct dating back to Neanderthals, seeing the woman he cared about wrapped up in something that belonged to him. As if the woman inside belonged to him, too. His weary body hummed with an electric response at just how feminine and delicate she seemed inside those ordinary, masculine clothes. Barefoot. No makeup to hide her smooth skin and wide, full mouth. Sleek, long hair glistening like the richest cup of coffee.

Yeah. He probably liked her in that shapeless black jacket a lot more than he should.

Shaking his head, Michael tucked in the corner of the fitted sheet near the headboard. It had been a helluva long day for him, too, to let some primitive, emotional reaction to her appearance lead his thoughts off track like that. "I take it you're not a night owl?"

"I prefer the morning sun." She was plaiting her damp hair into a loose braid and he had to force himself to look away from the unintentionally sensual display. "Too many memories of late nights and wasted days."

"I can't imagine coming back from the place where you were, Jillian."

She flicked the braid behind her back and crossed to the opposite side of the bed. "You make it sound like I did an amazing thing. I got into the party scene and used cocaine because I was so freaked out that my parents had died on their way to see me play an exhibition game. It's a wonder I ever graduated from high school."

He shot a pillow at her across the bed, which she deftly caught and set into place. "Yet you *did* graduate. You got a college degree and a master's in physical therapy. And you've been sober, what, ten years?"

"Eleven."

"I'd say helping others, especially the ones who are most needy, is your drug of choice now."

She grabbed the edge of the bright red top sheet and folded a neat hospital corner. "I would have said running and shootin' hoops was my regular fix. But I guess saving the world one person at a time keeps me out of trouble." Her relaxed, graceful movements stuttered to a halt as her green-eyed gaze darted over to his. "Well, sort of."

She hurried around the bed to complete the other corner, and plucked the bedspread out of his hands. "I'm just kind of going through a bad spell right now, with…Loverboy and Blake and Troy and…" She hugged the cover to her chest and laughed, but he couldn't detect any real humor. "I'm sorry that my problems have turned your life upside down, Michael. Sometimes I wish you never would have found that letter. I never meant to get you or Mike or Troy or anyone else hurt."

Michael pulled the cover right back and tossed it onto the bed. Something closer to the Neanderthal in him pushed aside rational thought. He snatched the front of the jacket she wore, an edge of the collar in each hand, and pulled her right to him. Close enough for toes to touch. Close enough for breaths to mingle. Far enough away that he could see deep into the expressive kaleidoscope of moss, jade and emerald in the irises of her eyes.

"I can't imagine you dealing with that bastard on your own. His actions are already escalating, and I've seen firsthand where that kind of diseased relationship leads." He smoothed the damp silk of her hair off her cheek. "No woman should be at any man's mercy like that."

"Michael, is this…?" She slid her hands around his wrists, eliciting sparks of heat against his skin. Those Irish eyes were so vivid, so vulnerable. "Is that the cop talking? Or the man? Because I really don't want to misread what's going on here."

He traced the edge of the bandage on her chin, carefully avoiding the neat row of stitches underneath. "I always thought we were the same guy. I want to protect you for Mike's sake. He needs you." He pressed his thumb against the soft pink swell of her lips and the desire to claim those beautiful lips throbbed inside him. "Sweetheart, I'm fifteen years older than you. But I'm sure not feeling like a daddy watching out for his little girl."

"I sure don't feel like a little girl around you." She smiled beneath his touch. "You're not who I would have thought I'd want. But I do. I can't help it. I do."

"You're good for my ego, Miss Legs." He stroked his thumb across her lips, denying himself the pleasure of touching them with his own. He needed to think here, not just react. This was more than lust he was feeling for Jillian, more than duty that had him making a bed for her under his roof. "But I never thought there'd be another woman in my life after Pam died. I don't know what to make of whatever's going on between us."

A tug on his wrist pulled his thumb away from its distracting exploration. "Do you feel like you're betraying her by feeling something for me?"

"No," he answered honestly. "I know that chapter of my life is over. I'll never forget her— she gave me my son and fifteen beautiful years of marriage—but I don't know what it is I feel for you. I don't want to get it wrong. You've got enough to cope with—hell, we both do. I don't want to complicate things more than they already are. I thought I was done with relationships, that I would be a cop and a dad for the rest of my life—and I was fine with that. But then you come smiling in and waking things up and making me think I'm not quite so—"

"Don't you dare say..." her face crinkled up in an adorable attempt to hide another yawn "...over the hill. See? You are in the prime of your life, Captain. I'm the one who can't keep up."

"It's two in the morning. Some old..." He saw the eyebrow of reprimand arch up and smiled. "Some *wise* man I am. Keeping you up talking when you need your rest." Fisting the jacket collar in both hands, he pulled her forward and pressed a kiss to her forehead. His lips lingered against her smooth, cool skin as he fought the magnetic desire to pull her body into his, to feel her supple curves aligning with his harder angles, to feel her generous spirit consume his closed-off heart and breathe life into it again. He kissed her again and pulled away, because that was what *she* needed right now. "I'm at the end of the hall if you need anything."

She wrapped her arms around her waist in a posture he was beginning to recognize as a tell for when she was feeling vulnerable. And it

made every instinct in him want to hold on tight
and shield her from whatever made her afraid
or unsure. But she needed protection right now,
a chance to recuperate. And as long as his head
wasn't in the right place, he wouldn't be any
good to her.

"I want to finish this conversation, Michael.
I think it could be very important…" another
yawn "…for both of us."

He felt disjointed, incomplete, keeping his
distance like this. He was a grown man—his
body could simmer with want and he could
walk away and deal with it. But his brain was a
different thing. He needed to think. He needed
to understand what he was feeling before he
could give her the answers she needed. "When
we're rested and thinking clearly. I promise.
Good night, Jillian."

"Good night."

Walking away from that wounded, worried
face was one of the hardest things Michael
had ever done.

SHE HADN'T HAD THE NIGHTMARE for a long
time. Try as she might to wake herself, Jillian's
body and mind were too tired, her emotions too
raw and unsettled, to will it away.

Jillian couldn't think clearly as she tumbled

through the doorway and landed in a heap on the floor. The room was dark, the smell was foul. Too much cologne couldn't mask the body odor and incense that reeked throughout the apartment.

The slam of a door jerked her to her senses. The hand on her arm jerked her to her feet. "Did you and your boyfriend help yourself to my stash?"

"No!"

Isaac Rush's hard fingers pinched her arms. His pockmarked face twisted with contempt. "He didn't pay, sugar. You're gonna have to."

"I don't have any money."

He picked her up and tossed her onto the bed like so much trash. "You think I'm giving it away for free here?"

"Isaac, no." Jillian scrambled to get away when he sat at the foot of the bed and kicked his shoes off. Her arms and legs tangled in the covers and she fought to free herself. "I don't do that. Blake said he paid you. I want to see Blake."

"Blake's already gone, sugar. Left you to take care of the bill." He reached out and touched her foot. She jerked it away and backed against the headboard. Isaac laughed as he crawled farther onto the bed. "That's not how a man takes care of his lady." Striking as quick as a snake, he grabbed her ankle and dragged her

back down on the bed. She kicked with her free foot, but he got hold of that ankle, too. And then she was flat on her back and he was on top of her. "I could set you up for life, baby, if you'd just spread those long legs and be with me."

"I don't... I don't want to." She shoved his face away from hers, kicked at his legs, twisted her knee.

Her shoe clipped his shin and he swore. He slapped her across the cheek. "Everybody pays!" The blow rang through her skull and brought tears to her eyes, killing the fight long enough for him to unzip her jeans. "One way or the other, everybody pays."

"Stop." She smacked at his shoulders and tried to roll him off her. She was vaguely aware of a door opening, of someone else entering the room.

"Sugar, we've got something special. You know we do."

She was more aware of his hand tugging down her pants. Jillian clawed at his wrists. "Stop!"

A shadow loomed up behind Isaac, and suddenly he flew across the room and she was free. Blinded by tears and panic and darkness, she could only hear the scuffle, the grunts and protests as she scrambled off the bed and fastened her jeans. Her rescuer grabbed a syringe from the nightstand and followed Isaac into the corner. It had never been this bad before. She'd never been this terrified.

Before she could even think to run, the black man who'd gotten rid of Isaac was back. Mr. Lynch. Oh, God. Did he want something from her, too? He grabbed her arm, but Jillian's scream was quickly muffled by the clamp of his hand over her mouth.

He'd dragged her all the way to the lobby doors before he let her speak again. "What are you doing? Where are you taking me? Where's Blake?"

"That pig of a boyfriend got you into this mess. I'm gettin' you out." He threw open the door and pulled her onto the front stoop. "I never believed it was right to pay like that. You ain't even legal age yet. You're too good for this life. Too young." He shoved her away and turned for the door. "Go home, girl."

Jillian ran back. "I won't leave without Blake. Isaac will hurt him when he finds out I took a hit and didn't pay."

"You're not paying that way." He caught her by the arm and hauled her all the way down the stairs. "Your boyfriend's long gone. Isaac's my problem. You don't ever come back here."

"But—"

"You don't belong here, girl." When she didn't move, he pushed her away. "Get out of here!"

Once Jillian found her feet, she ran. She ended up on her brother Eli's doorstep.

The next day she was in court, her skin crawling with a terrible need.

Then she was in her small room at the Boatman Clinic, going through withdrawal. In Dr. Randolph's office for meeting after meeting, and talking and hugging and healing.

For a moment, Jillian breathed fresh air. Her body relaxed. She rolled over in the bed.

And then the merciless talons from her past dug into her mind and sucked her back down into the nightmare.

She couldn't escape. Not ever. Not really. The fear was the same, the helplessness real.

Red carnations were raining down all around her, stinging her sinuses with their perfumey scent. The horrible sound of fists pounding on bruised and broken flesh spasmed through her body. A man's voice whispered disturbing, indistinct words in her ears about love and need and being his. Then he just said her name.

Over and over again.

"Stop it." Jillian thrashed from side to side,

bound by the words, tortured by the promise behind them. "Stop it!"

And then she was running. Pushing her way through the sea of flowers and running through the darkness. The voice pursued her.

Jillian. Jillian.

"No!" she cried out. A light flashed on, searing through her retinas and bringing her pain. "Please, no."

With light came a new scene, more grisly and frightening and confining than the last.

She was trapped on an elevator now, the walls and floor red with blood, not flowers. A dark figure lay slumped in the corner, its moans of pain matching Jillian's own mewling cries.

This was her. Her fate. Her punishment.

Jillian. Jillian.

"Leave me alone!"

The elevator doors opened, but there was no place to run, nowhere to hide. A faceless man walked in, carrying a bouquet of bright red flowers. "You're not alone. I want you. I love you."

"No." She backed into the corner, raised her hands to fight.

"I love you." The flowers had vanished and his hands were on her now.

"No."

"I love you, Jillian." His hands crept around her throat.

She struck out at his featureless face. "No!"

He raised his fist into the air. "Love me."

"No."

She felt his rage like a fist in her gut. "Love me!"

"No!"

"Love me!"

"Jillian!" Hands were truly on her now, battling with her flying fists and twisting body as her screams tore through her. "Jillian, wake up!"

"No!" Jillian panted for breath. Sweat beaded between her breasts and at the small of her back.

Her eyes focused on the light from the lamp on the bedside table. Then coal-black hair with sprinkles of silver registered. Her wrists were bound against her pillows, her body pinned in a spread-eagle position. She saw broad shoulders, an unshaven chin and midnight-blue eyes.

"Michael?"

"Are you with me?" Those piercing eyes scanned every nuance of her changing expression as she found her way back to the football-themed bedroom in Michael Cutler's house.

As she found her way back to the blessed

security of Michael watching over her. "Michael!"

He released her as soon as he knew she was herself. As he pulled away the covers that wreathed her body, she pushed herself up and threw her arms around his neck.

"Michael, it was awful."

"Shh." He absorbed her momentum, catching her around the waist and falling backward onto the bed, pulling her to rest on top of him. He smoothed the sticky hair away from her temple and pressed a kiss there. "It was a bad dream. Just a dream. You're safe."

She shifted her ear to the reassuring thump of his heart and turned her nose into a crisp mat of sooty curls and the clean, familiar scent of his warm skin underneath. He loosened her hair and sifted his fingers through it, then slipped his hand beneath the weight of it to palm the nape of her neck. Jillian wasn't sure how long they lay together that way, with Michael gently rocking her back and forth, feathering kisses against her hair and neck and down across the jut of her shoulder.

When she finally sighed an unfettered breath and wiped the remnants of tears from her swollen, hot eyes, he shifted his grip to frame her face and tilt her eyes up to meet his.

A hint of a smile played on his lips. "You gonna clock me again?"

"Did I really hit you?" He tapped the edge of his jaw and her gaze flew to the spot. A red mark. She felt her own cheeks turn a similar color. "Oh, no. I'm sorry."

She made a graceless attempt to find a place to put her knees and climb off him. But he foiled her escape by simply smiling and rolling onto his side, dumping her onto the bed beside him and throwing his leg over both of hers to let her know he had no interest in breaking the contact between them.

And there was plenty of contact. Lots and lots of places where their bodies touched or the thin barrier of her tank top and panties, and his black boxer shorts left little to the imagination. Jillian let Michael's deep, drowsy voice mesmerize her while her body took note of all the glorious, intimate contrasts between them.

"That's why I held you down. Hope I didn't scare you. Just protecting myself." The crisp texture of hair along his muscular thigh and calf tickled her smoother skin like the soft lick of a cat's tongue. His left hand had settled with a possessive claim around her bottom, trapping her soft feminine center between the heat of his palm and the unyielding hardness of his body.

"You scared me plenty enough for both of us. Your screams woke me. You were really fighting a demon of some kind. Do you need to talk about it?"

"I haven't had the nightmares for a long time," she admitted, feeling the dark shadows of memory and imagination being chased back into the corners of her mind by her own growing response to the heat and strength of the man holding her. Jillian rubbed her palms across the angles of his neck, chest, shoulders and arms, waking a primal feminine power inside her to feel his muscles jump and bunch beneath each stroke of her hand.

"You were exhausted. That doesn't help." He shifted his position slightly, perhaps to hide the growing evidence of his arousal nudging against her thigh. His blue eyes demanded her attention and she willingly tilted her face to read the promise shining there. "Were you thinking about what happened tonight with Rush and Lynch? They're both in jail tonight. Rivers is in the hospital, with a guard watching him. They can't hurt you."

"I know." Her breathing quickened when his gaze dropped to her lips and his eyes dilated and darkened. "It was just some of the horrors of my past getting mixed up with everything that's going on now. Tonight. The letters. Mrs. Anthony. What you said about things getting worse."

"I shouldn't have scared you like that." He blinked, moved his hands to a more neutral position, which turned out not to be very neutral at all because his chest brushed against the pearls of her tight nipples, sending a burst of electric energy from that point of contact straight down to her womb, making every point of contact suddenly several degrees hotter. "I can be…" he swallowed hard and she watched the movement all the way down the column of his throat to see that his chest was rising and falling in an unsteady rhythm, too "…pretty harsh about making a point."

"No. I want to be smart about this—how I handle things." Jillian squeezed her eyes shut, fighting to control the warring impulses inside her. Fear and comfort. Nightmares and light. Past and present. Patience and desire. Following the lonely existence her choices had sentenced her to and following her heart.

"Jillian." He sensed it, too. The hand at her waist squeezed almost to the point of pain as he struggled to maintain control. "I haven't wanted anything like this for a long time. But I'm smart enough to know it can't just be something physical. I don't want to get this any more complicated. I don't want to make it worse for you."

"You can't." She stretched up to kiss his lips, feeling both hope and fear as he caught hers and tried to cling to them as she pulled away. "At the hospital, you said you needed something from me. I need something, too. I need to feel. I need to know that I'm okay, that some part of me is still normal. For a little while, anyway. Michael." She rubbed her palm across his prickly jaw and begged him to understand. "Please."

"Yeah." He dipped his head to reclaim her lips. Once. Twice. Again. "I need that, too." His dark eyes told her the truth. "I need you."

And then there were no more words. He framed her face between his hands and took her mouth in a deep, fiery kiss. Jillian ran her fingers behind his neck and over his hair, opening herself to him in every way possible. What he wanted, she bestowed. What she needed, he gave.

When he skimmed her tank top off over her head, she gasped in delight at every sure sweep of his hand against her feverish skin. When he laved his tongue around the pebbled tip of her breast, she moaned at the frictional caress. When he opened his hot, wet mouth over its aching mate, she bucked beneath him.

His hands were in her hair, at her hips, on her thighs and in the swollen, needy thatch between.

With every touch, an ember was born inside her. With every kiss, it burst into flame. She was molten, fluid, alive with Michael Cutler.

When he moved on top of her, pressing her body into the mattress beneath the good, masculine weight of his, Jillian welcomed him as he slipped inside. Michael propped himself up on his elbows so he could soothe the waiting sparks with a kiss on her panting, parted lips. Jillian wrapped her long legs around his hips and locked them together. She wrapped her arms around his shoulders to hold on for the ride. She wrapped herself up in the power of that deep midnight gaze and let him see the flames of need and gratitude and love shining in her own eyes.

She pulled him down to her when he began to move inside her. He thrust his fingers into her hair, burying his nose against her neck as he plunged into her throbbing heat.

Jillian came and cried out and cried out again as the fire exploded deep inside and radiated through her in wave after wave of heat. A moment later, Michael's hands fisted in her hair and he poured out his own release deep inside her.

Sometime later, while Jillian dozed on the pillow of Michael's shoulder, he picked her up and carried her down the hall to his own bedroom and tucked her into the four-poster bed. She murmured a drowsy protest that her own legs were working and he shushed her with a kiss.

He climbed into the bed behind her and spooned his body to hers, pulling the covers up over them both. "Sleep, sweetheart." Brushing her tangled hair off her face, he whispered a promise against her ear. "You're safe."

Jillian sank into a deep, decadent sleep. Together, they'd burned the nightmares out of her system and replaced them with the sweet dreams and fierce gift of Michael Cutler's healing touch.

MICHAEL TOOK THE STAIRS two at a time, carrying a tray filled with two mugs of coffee and a package of chocolate fudge toaster pastries. Clearly, he was going to have to hit the grocery store if he was going to be keeping two teenage boys in his house.

But when he opened the bedroom door—and quickly closed it behind him again—food was no longer the first thing on his mind.

Jillian was standing in front of the bathroom mirror, wrapped in nothing but a towel. She had her long brown ponytail draped over one shoulder and was using his comb to smooth the tangles of their late-night tussle from her hair. "Good morning."

Obviously, she'd opened the door to let the steam from her shower escape—not to give him a midmorning peep show that revved up his energy more than that first cup of coffee he'd already drunk. So he made a valiant effort to turn his head from each stroke of her hand and carry on a normal conversation. "Good morning. Coffee?"

"Please."

He set the tray on the dresser and brought her a mug and one of the pastries. "Sorry. Breakfast pickings are pretty slim today. The boys have already wolfed down the cold pizza and grazed through whatever they could find in the cabinets."

She laughed as she set down the comb and picked up the steaming mug. Her sniff and sip and resulting "mmm" were a little like heaven for him, too. "That's good. Thanks."

Tactical error. In addition to miles of smooth, tanned skin stretching over sleek curves, the humid air in the smaller room was heavy with the scent of soap and Jillian herself. But he could handle this morning-after awkwardness if he didn't look directly at her or her reflection in the mirror.

But his effort to avoid her eyes left him staring at the long purplish bruise that adorned her collarbone this morning. He reached out and touched it gently with his forefinger, and then touched another bruise on her arm, and another. He bit back the furious desire to count each of the marks on her arms and legs, and who knew where else, from her tumble down the stairs with Blake Rivers last night.

She seemed to think the risks she took were some kind of penance she owed for a rebellious youth. But no woman, especially a warrior as brave and stubborn and giving as Jillian Masterson, deserved to be hurt by the very scum of the world she tried so hard to help.

Something about the stillness of his posture, or his inability to move his gaze from the black-and-blue swelling at her knee, must have betrayed him. She cupped the side of his clean-shaven jaw and turned him to face her. "Michael."

"Do they hurt much?"

"I'm okay. My chin's a little tender," she admitted, "but I'm okay. I'm better inside, too, now. Thanks to you."

He caught her hand and pressed a kiss to her

palm before pulling away. *Lighten the mood, Mr. Gloom and Doom.*

Turning to rest his hip on the vanity beside her, Michael pulled out the slick material that he'd stuffed into the back pocket of his jeans. "Here." He handed her the pair of basketball shorts that Mike had picked out for her. "I thought you might like to wear something besides those blood-spattered khakis today."

Mention blood. Right. That's how to move beyond that raw feeling of wanting to do some damage to the people who'd threatened and hurt her.

He'd have to learn to count on Jillian's resiliency. "Mike doesn't mind me wearing them?"

"He offered."

"I'll have to thank him." She pulled the shorts on beneath her towel, hiding a few more inches of leg, and tilted her mouth into a frown. "You're still going to take me back to my apartment to get my own things, right? I called Lulu at work, and she said she'd get Dylan to cover for me until lunch. But I can't wear these when I do show up."

"Relax. I'm off the clock today. I'll take you."

"And I'd like to get my own wheels back."

"Your SUV will be safe enough on the KCPD lot." She propped a hand on her hip and turned to argue, but he didn't give her the chance. "Besides, I'm not letting you go anywhere without an armed escort. Today, I'm your man. I'll take you home, take you to work, take you to wherever. But I am not letting you out of my sight until we, *a,* have a better idea of who Loverboy might be and what his intentions are, and, *b,* I know you're not going to run off and put yourself in unnecessary danger again trying to help someone else."

The frown curved into a wry smile. "That's awfully bossy of you."

Michael sat back on the vanity top and crossed his arms over the front of his black T-shirt. "I like being in charge."

"So I gather." She rested a gentle hand on his forearm. "That's an awful lot of responsibility, Michael."

"I can handle it."

"You probably can," she agreed. "But that doesn't mean you have to be in control all the time. Cut yourself some slack."

Right. When Michael Cutler lost his focus, he got off his game. And that's when people got tossed down a flight of stairs. Or shot by an obsessive ex-boyfriend.

As if he was going to let any of that happen again.

"Get dressed."

She arched a rebellious eyebrow. "Yes, sir."

When Jillian turned to pull on her bra and tank top and lose the towel altogether, Michael went back into the bedroom to retrieve his own cup of coffee and try to get his head firmly back into cop mode, which meant putting some distance between them.

He took a bite of cold pastry and chewed while he slid his holster and badge onto his belt and secured his Glock. Maybe he needed his uniform and body armor on to get last night and the memory of Jillian's sexy, fragrant hair and supple body flying apart all around him out of his head. When Jillian padded out of the bathroom and went straight for the black KCPD jacket he'd loaned her last night, and shrugged it around her shoulders, he knew he was never going to be able to completely separate his thirst for the fire Jillian brought into his life from his need to protect her.

But he'd find a way to get the job done. "I got the boys up without any problem and got their day started," he reported.

"I could have helped with that."

"You needed your sleep."

"And you didn't?"

She was tying on her tennis shoes now. Her

sporty attire and lack of makeup made her look even younger. But the legs? His jacket? His Neanderthalic hormones were kicking in again. Nope. He wasn't tired at all.

He gave up on the idea of breakfast and keeping his distance and crossed to where she was sitting on the edge of the bed. Pulling her to her feet, Michael wrapped her in his arms and covered her mouth with a kiss. He teased her lips and taunted and tasted, and then got dead serious about claiming all of the eager response she offered when she stretched up on tiptoe and wound her arms around his neck, running her hands along his nape and hair in that needy, graspy way that had ripped away the last of his defenses last night.

When he felt the bedpost at her back, he realized he'd been shamelessly driving his hips against her, and finally tore his mouth from hers. His heart was pounding, his breathing was ragged, his jeans were tight. But he rested his forehead against hers and pulled back, desperately needing the cool air that flowed between them.

Apparently, the only way he was going to know peace with this woman was to hold her in his arms 24/7. But his peace of mind wasn't her problem. He looked down into her upturned eyes, thinking she knew exactly just how far out of his control his life was spinning since he'd invited her into it.

But that wasn't a fact he was ready to admit. Not when he needed to keep it all together to protect her from Loverboy.

He turned away from those knowing green eyes and swatted her bottom before heading for the door. "Say good morning to the boys. I'll meet you out front in my truck."

HIS CLOTHES WERE WRINKLED and a little ripe after his long night. A bite of lunch would be nice. But he wasn't leaving his parking place until he knew Jillian had come home and seen the gift he'd left for her.

He knew the policeman had taken her to the hospital, that she'd be cleaned up and cared for there. He'd wanted to be at the medical center this morning to see for himself that she hadn't been seriously injured, but he'd been unavoidably detained.

What happened last night couldn't be allowed to happen again. Sweet, brave Jillian in the wrong part of town, outnumbered and outgunned. She was fortunate that her injuries hadn't been life threatening. A tumble down those old stairs could have broken her neck.

She could have been hit, strangled, or shot by a desperate man so full of himself that he didn't care about the danger he put others in.

But *he* cared. He cared that Jillian was safe. That she wouldn't be hurt like that again. He'd seen to it personally that that bastard would never hurt her again.

She'd be so pleased. It was the least he could do for the woman he loved. It was just a taste of all he was willing to do for her.

He pulled down the visor over the steering wheel and touched the picture of her he'd clipped there. "I'll take care of you, Jilly. Whenever you need me, I'll be here for you. One day you'll understand just how much I love—"

A black pickup truck passed him on the road and turned into the parking lot of Jillian's apartment building. He'd been concerned that he hadn't seen her dark blue SUV in the lot, but now it looked as though the officer who'd driven her to the hospital last night had also picked her up this morning.

He didn't like that. Didn't like other men doing favors for her. Last night, he'd allowed it. It was quicker than getting an ambulance to her, and he'd had no other choice but to let her go. But today…

Suspicion and loathing burned a hole in his

empty belly. He kissed his fingertip, then shook it in reprimand at the smiling image looking back at him, before closing the visor and starting the engine. She shouldn't be trying his patience like this, not when he'd been so worried for her. Not when he'd done so much.

After the black pickup pulled into a parking place, he turned into the lot himself and slowly circled around, keeping an eye on Jillian. When the driver got out, he tapped on the brake and laughed at his foolishness. It was that old cop, the one with gray in his hair. He never should have suspected Jillian of betraying him. Naturally, she'd feel safe with a father figure like that. Considering where she'd come from, all she'd endured and overcome, she probably found great comfort in the paternal asexuality of Graybeard there.

He waited and watched as the senior cop opened her door and walked her around to the back of his truck.

And then he saw that they were holding hands. They laughed. She tugged on the man's hand and he turned. Jillian touched the side of the old man's face and drew him down for a kiss.

He sat up straight. His blood boiled in his veins. The tramp! Giving her lovin' out for free to every man she met when he'd been faithful and true to her for longer than she deserved. He loved her because she was sweet and innocent and his.

"I love you, Jillian." He shifted his foot to the accelerator. "*I* love you."

Chapter Ten

Jillian had her keys out of her pocket as soon as Michael turned the truck into the parking lot of her apartment building. But she wasn't about to let this conversation end with him claiming that he was perfectly fine—that there were no lingering regrets about the outcome of the hostage crisis at the bank yesterday, that he wasn't as perplexed by the yin and yang of their relationship as she was, and that everything was peachy keen and under control in his world.

"I know it's hard." She reached across the seat and tugged at the sleeve of the pullover sweater he wore, wanting to offer comfort as well as understanding. "But acceptance does come. With enough time."

He took his hand off the wheel long enough to squeeze her hand. "Have you moved past feeling guilty about the things you did all those years ago in No-Man's Land?" When she pulled away at the uncomfortable change of topic, he let her. "I know you understand guilt and regret the way I do, Jillian. Have you really moved on and left all that behind you?"

"Most of the time."

"And when you can't?"

"Like with you and the shooting yesterday?" Uh-huh. She could tell by the tension in his knuckles around the steering wheel that the incident was still weighing heavily on him. "I'm blessed with family. And a good therapist who still listens to me every now and then when I need him."

"I tell my men to talk to the police psychologist when they need to." Michael pulled into a parking space and turned off the engine, turning in his seat to face her. "Pam used to do that for me. Just listen. Before she got sick. I wouldn't dump on her after that. And I won't unload on Mike."

Had he talked to anyone beyond a grief counselor since his wife's death? Pam Cutler had been blessed to have such a stalwart man by her side as she succumbed to cancer. But maintaining control of his emotions didn't necessarily mean Michael was dealing with them. "Maybe you should try opening up with Mike a little. He's sixteen. He's trying to be a man. But he's been through a lot. Maybe if he sees you opening up about some of your fears and frustrations, he will, too."

"Damn, if that doesn't make sense." His eyes narrowed as if he couldn't quite believe what he'd heard. Or couldn't believe he was actually considering taking her advice. With a shake of his head he got out of the truck and circled around to meet her. He took her hand and walked her toward the building. "How'd you get so wise for someone so young?"

Jillian halted at the back of his truck and tugged on his hand to turn him. "I'm twenty-eight, Michael, not a child."

"Don't I know it. This might be a hell of a lot easier if you were."

With a smile, she cupped his strong jaw and rewarded his open-mindedness with a kiss. She didn't intend to make it easy for him to dismiss her very real, very grown-up love for him. "You can dump on me anytime," she whispered. "And keep talking to Mike. Give him a chance. Give yourself—"

She heard the whine of tires spinning to find traction.

"Jillian!" A powerful engine roared in her ears an instant before Michael's arm clamped down like a vise around her waist and they went flying through the air. A green monster barreled past in a rush of wind, spitting gravel that nipped at her skin a split second before they hit the ground and skidded across the asphalt. Michael tucked her head against his chest and they rolled until the front wheel of his truck slammed them to a stop.

"Stay down!" Michael scrambled to his feet, gun drawn, and ran after the speeding car.

"Michael, no!"

Ignoring new bumps and dizziness and shock, Jillian sat up, curling her knees to her chest and huddling next to the wheel as she braced for the sound of a gunshot. Tires screeched. She cringed. Horns honked. Michael cursed. No shots. Thank God. And then the only sounds she heard were her heart pounding against her ribs and the crunch of footsteps hurrying back toward her.

"This is Captain Cutler, SWAT Team One."

As soon as she saw him turn the corner between his truck and the car beside it, Jillian pushed to her feet. His gun was back in its holster and his cop face was on as he tipped his cell phone away from his mouth and took her hand to help her stand. "You're bleeding." He nodded down at her knee. "You okay?"

"Good enough." She stooped over to brush the debris from her skinned-up knee and idly noted she had a matching pair of bum knees now, not unlike her childhood as a tomboy. From this angle she also noted the tear in the sleeve of Michael's sweater and the scrape along his elbow underneath. "You?"

"I'll live." He hugged her right into his chest, blocking her between the vehicles, as he turned his attention back to the dispatcher on his cell phone. "I know *green* and *car* isn't much to go on. Run the partial plate to see what you get. Keep me posted if traffic patrol pulls over anyone that matches. Cutler out."

He clipped his phone back on his belt. Keeping her tucked against his side, Michael headed across the lawn, making a beeline for the front door even as his eyes scouted in every direction around them. "Let's get you inside in case he decides to come back for round two."

Jillian had no problem hanging on and picking up the pace. "Do you think that was him? Loverboy?"

"Oh, I know it was."

"Did you see his face?"

Michael stood at her back while she unlocked the security door and led him inside. "I was too busy trying not to get hit. We almost had a head-on collision at the entrance. He was gone by the time I got the other car clear."

"No one else was hurt?"

"Not this time." Despite her nightmare, they went straight for the elevator. Once inside, he continued to hold her and Jillian rested her head against his shoulder, feeling the adrenaline of fear and danger starting to wane. "A few days ago, you said you felt like someone was watching you. Maybe he's been around here all along and I was too blind to see it. Did you recognize the car? Do you think you may have seen it before?"

She waited for the doors to open on the third floor before she answered. "I didn't get that good of a look—just a blur of green as it flew past us. It was a lighter color. Almost mossy. I'm trying to think of anyone I know who has a car that color…" She saw the envelope tacked to her door at the end of the hallway. "Michael."

Dread rooted her to the spot for one moment. Outrage sent her running down the hall the next.

But Michael was there, snatching her wrist out of the way as she reached for it. "Don't touch it. I want to know how he got inside the building. Do you have gloves inside?" She nodded. "Get 'em."

Under Michael's careful eye, she took the envelope inside her apartment. Self-adhesive seal. No stamp. No postmark. Just her name typed across the front.

While Michael paced from window to locked door and back to the sink to wet down some paper towels, Jillian opened the envelope. A strip of pressed gold and nickel slipped out and clunked onto the kitchen table. She flipped it over to see the *R* engraved on the opposite side. A money clip. Was it another unwanted gift? It wasn't her initial and she didn't want it any more than she'd wanted those flowers. Was it something she was supposed to recognize? She unfolded the letter. Maybe she'd find answers there.

My dearest Jillian,

Are you safe? Are you well? You've changed the lock and now I can't get in to help you. It's all right, my love. I know you're afraid. I forgive you.

I was frightened myself last night. For you. It broke my heart to see how brave you were. You don't belong in Isaac Rush's world. You never did. To know that you would risk your life to help someone who doesn't appreciate you the way I do sickens me. You have a noble, beautiful spirit that I've come to know so well, and I admire your dedication to helping others. But please, please, please—don't let your past destroy you. It would kill me to see you hurt by another man.

The blood drained down to her toes and she sank into the nearest chair as she read on.

I love you. More than my own life. More than my own freedom. And I know you have feelings for me, too, that we can never express. You don't have to say you love me. Because of your brave heart and generous spirit, I know you care.

I will treasure the beautiful gift you are every day, even when we're apart. I will honor that gift. And I will protect the love you have for me inside you.

I have always been there for you, Jilly. I'm here for you now. Here is proof of my love for you. I've seen to it personally that the man who hurt you last night will never hurt you again.

I'm keeping you safe from the horrors of your life. I will always keep you safe. I

know that some day when we are together, in this world or the next, you will thank me.
Until then I am forever,
Yours

"What has he done now?" Jillian swiped at the tears burning her eyes and looked down to the man kneeling beside her, cleaning her scraped-up knee. "I don't understand."

Michael set aside the towels and quickly read the note. "He was there last night. In No-Man's Land. He must have seen what happened to you in Troy's building."

"But what does he mean, 'never hurt you again'? Who does that freak think he's protecting me from?" *Oh, no.* She picked up the money clip on the table and traced the *R* with her gloved finger. *R. Rivers.* He'd used her as a shield to escape from Isaac and had pulled her down the stairs with him in his haste to get away. "Blake." She leaped to her feet, ignoring the pain of the sudden movement. "We have to get to the hospital. We have to help Blake."

"Jillian. Jillian!"

But she was already out the door. Already afraid she was too late.

MICHAEL'S PHONE CALLS to the Truman Medical Center and then to Edward Kincaid had given him the grim news long before he and Jillian arrived at the hospital. Not that she'd take his word and let him spare her the trip. She had to see it for herself.

Blake Rivers was dead.

The hospital room was about as cold and pristine as the anger beating in Michael's heart. He didn't care one whit about Rivers, but he cared a great deal about the stony-faced woman wrapped up in his jacket and hugging herself beside him.

Jillian shouldn't have to be here. She shouldn't have to see this. It wasn't the most disturbing D.B. Michael had ever dealt with. But the body was still in rigor mortis, indicating how violently and helplessly Blake Rivers had suffered right before his death earlier that morning.

Edward had gotten there first, to cordon off the room and take statements from the staff, who hadn't noticed anyone or anything out of the ordinary until Blake's monitors had stopped and signaled them at the floor desk. Edward hadn't been able to convince Jillian to wait out in the corridor to let them work. His wife, Dr. Holly Masterson-Kincaid, was the medical examiner in charge of the initial analysis of the body. She hadn't been able to convince her sister to leave the potential crime scene, either.

What chance did Michael think he had to get her out of here without upsetting her even further?

"Sweetheart…"

She jumped when he spoke and huddled even deeper inside the collar of his jacket. But her feet wouldn't budge. In the end, Michael opted to simply hold on to her.

"And you can rule out accidental death?" Edward asked his wife, taking Michael's cue to stand at the end of the bed to block the worst of the scene from Jillian's view. "He did have a head injury."

"Not a life-threatening one, according to his charts." Though not as tall as her younger sister, Holly Masterson-Kincaid had the same leggy figure and dark hair that Jillian had, as well as that familiar twist to her mouth when she was deep in thought. Like now, as she bent over Rivers's hospital bed with her flashlight and inspected the body. "The facial petechiae indicate suffocation, but there are no ligature marks or other bruising around his neck." She studied the fingernails on one hand before carefully sliding a protective paper bag over the hand. "There's trace here. And some of these bruises are newer than the others. He struggled against something. Or someone." Energized by a sudden discovery, Holly circled behind her husband and approached the body from the opposite side. With a steady balance between flashlight and plastic tweezers, she plucked a tiny filament from Rivers's mouth and held it up. "Probably the person who held a pillow over his face."

After sliding the filament into a tiny envelope, Holly walked across the room. She hugged Jillian around the shoulders, and held on even tighter when she tried to shrug off her supportive touch. "I'm sorry, hon. It's definitely murder."

"I knew it."

Thank God she was responding to someone. A tear trickled down Jillian's cheek as she turned her eyes to her sister.

"Now can I get you out of here?" Holly asked.

With a nod, Jillian allowed Holly to lead her into the hallway and down to a row of seats. Michael followed and sat on the opposite side, wishing Jillian would hold on to his hand the same way she'd latched on to her sister's.

After a drink of water from Edward and a chance to compose herself, Jillian turned to Holly. "This is my fault."

"How do you figure that? Edward told me

about the letters and the break-in. I would have thought Blake was a prime suspect—he never did seem to get over you breaking up with him."

"Can't say I'm sorry to see the SOB go." Edward sat on the arm of Holly's chair, resting his palm on her shoulder and taking her hand when she reached up to find his. "Do you know how many possession charges he's had over the years? They were all pled out or dismissed. He was spoiled and selfish and never good enough for you, kiddo."

"It doesn't matter who Blake was. Don't you get it? *I'm* the reason he's dead. First Troy Anthony's grandmother. Now this? Nobody look cross-eyed at me—he'll probably come after you, too." She turned to Michael, digging her fingers into the sleeve of his sweater, begging him to understand. "What if Mike throws a temper tantrum during a therapy session? Or you…" She reached up to cup his face and the tremors he felt in her normally confident touch nearly broke his heart.

"Jillian." He spread his hand over hers, warming her, comforting her, wishing he could tell her everything would be all right.

"I couldn't handle it if something happened to you or Mike." She turned to Holly and

Edward, including them in her plea. "To any of you."

When she faced Michael again, she sat up straight and breathed in deeply. The tears had dried, the shaking had stopped. All good signs that she was feeling more like her old self again after the triple shock of the attempt on her life, the letter and Blake's death. Still, an uneasy feeling stirred in Michael's gut. He knew that determined glint in her eye. He wasn't going to like what she had to say.

"I want to meet this guy."

"Absolutely not."

"Bad idea," Edward echoed.

"Jilly, no."

"Three votes to one." Michael pushed aside his gut reaction of stark, crazy fear for her, and stated the facts in his most authoritative tone. "That bastard tried to kill you today. Everything he's done has gotten more dangerous and more personal. You are not going to seek this guy out. You are not going to contact him. You are not going to set yourself up as some kind of bait to smoke him out. We'll get him. Without putting you in more danger. I promise."

"I don't want to wind up like Daphne Mullins. She was a victim. I won't be. I want to meet this guy and tell him to his face he has no idea what…love is." Her gaze drifted away to a nebulous point beyond his shoulder, then snapped back into focus. "Jilly."

"What is it?" Michael asked, sensing something very important had just clicked together in her brain. And it had nothing to do with his warnings to keep her safe.

"He calls me Jilly." She turned to her sister. "Sorry, Holly, but it's not my favorite nickname. Mom and Dad used to call me that. It makes me feel like a kid."

"So…?"

She raised her gaze to Michael. He understood. She was already zeroing in on this Loverboy bastard, and he couldn't do a damn thing to stop her.

"I'm making a list of everyone who calls me Jilly."

"SHE CAN'T BE LEFT ALONE. Ever. That's all there is to it."

Michael paced in his office at home, listening to the grim recording Edward Kincaid had brought over after he and Holly had gone back to Jillian's apartment to pack a bag of her things.

The messages recorded on Jillian's answering machine had started with a relatively benign

"I'm so worried. Are you okay?" and had progressed to the definite threat of "You freaking tramp! After all I've done for you, you aren't even the least bit grateful?"

"How many messages did you say he left?" Michael asked.

"Lucky thirteen. The frequency of calls is harassment enough." Edward's expression looked as murderously grim as Michael felt. "Holly's already called Eli. He's on a flight back to K.C. first thing in the morning. I can get my brothers to help keep an eye on her when they're off the clock."

"My team will, too."

"But this is Jillian Masterson we're talking about. Stubborn as they come," Edward pointed out. "Unless you know some sweet-talk trick that I never learned, sir, she's not going to hole up in your house indefinitely while we try to ID the guy."

Michael tuned out the next "Jilly, I'm sorry. You know I love you. I didn't mean…" recording and sat in the leather chair behind his desk, leaning forward to where Edward sat on the opposite side. He might outrank Edward at KCPD, but there were familial concerns he needed to respect. "Are you and Holly okay with her staying here?"

Edward scratched at the late night stubble lining his scarred jaw before he nodded. "Like I said, stubborn. If this is where Jillian feels safe, then this is where we want her to stay. Your experience with witness protection and running special weapons and tactics means you're probably the best man for the job, anyway. But you know she's going after this guy. She wants to maintain her regular routine so that we don't scare him off. She thinks she's protecting us."

Yeah. That had been a pointless argument that had lasted all the way home from the hospital. The only way to truly make Jillian and the people around her safe was to move faster and think smarter than Loverboy. "Any suspects we can bring in for questioning?"

"Isaac Rush and his man Lynch both posted bond this morning. I vote for one of them as the perp in the car with the death wish. They both had history with Blake Rivers." Michael liked Edward's methodical approach to discussing a case, and wondered what his secret was for detaching his emotions from an investigation that hit so close to home. "Could be one of them had another reason for silencing Rivers, and is using this stalking thing to cover up the real motive.

We're trying to trace their movements since their release from lockup this morning."

"You think terrorizing Jillian has been a setup to mask the motive for Rivers's murder?" Michael didn't like that scenario any better. "Are Rush and Lynch smart enough to plan out a hit that far in advance?"

"I'm just throwing possibilities out there. Holly told me that Lynch *rescued* Jillian back when she was a teenager—kept her from being assaulted by Rush. Maybe he's got some kind of savior complex with her. In his eyes he's taking care of her still."

"That would fit with what I overheard in the stairwell at Troy Anthony's building. She was pleading with Lynch to let her go *again.*"

"Of course, if Rush was the one attacking her—"

"He doesn't have feelings for her." A drug dealer who still had a thing for the woman he'd gone after when she was an underaged teen? The idea curdled Michael's stomach. "He's a businessman."

"One who'd take Rivers out if he thought Blake was conducting business on his turf. He's not above using Jillian, or anyone else, to maintain his power." Another message from the answering machine tape began to play. "That son of a bitch."

"…death is the only way. My love for you is pure and lasting. I can't allow you to mock my feelings for you again. I won't abide that kind of cruelty. I'm ready to give you the opportunity to show me that your love runs just as deep." And if it didn't? Michael's hands curled into fists at his sides. "I'm forever yours, Jilly. Forever."

So Edward Kincaid wasn't any more inured to the vile filth Loverboy was spouting about Jillian than he was. Every curse Edward uttered resonated deep inside his bones as Michael walked over to the tape player and shut it off. "She doesn't hear this tape, understood?"

Edward caught the cassette when Michael tossed it to him. He tucked the tape inside his jacket pocket and stood. "What if she can identify the voice?"

Michael shook his head. "It's raspy and distorted on the tape. Either he's pretty inebriated or he's intentionally masking it. I won't put her through listening to those for no reason."

"There's no sense dumping the numbers on her cell phone, either. They're easier to trace. He'd be too smart to leave a number there. And we haven't had any luck narrowing down an ID on the green car, either. This guy has *anonymous* down to an art."

How did they trip up a guy that clever? One who knew enough about Jillian—where she worked, where she lived, where she went to help her patients like Troy Anthony—to avoid showing up on the radar anywhere? Michael splayed his hands, racking his brain for answers. "How do we get this guy to show himself? What's his weakness?"

With a soft knock at the door, he had his answer.

Jillian walked in.

Michael's heart flip-flopped inside his chest. He'd already lost Pam. He'd nearly lost his son. Both, to events beyond his control. And he'd been powerless.

He couldn't lose anyone else he loved on his watch. He couldn't do it. It almost hurt his eyes to look at Jillian and feel this way.

Bait.

"I'm ready to give you the opportunity to show me that your feelings run just as deep."

Death.

How could he ever risk Jillian's life? Even if that was the only way they could draw Loverboy out and shut him down for good, how could he risk losing her?

Jillian's green eyes narrowed as they met his across the room. She sensed something—something Michael couldn't yet put into words—and he turned away to needlessly straighten the items on his desk.

But when her sister came in behind her, the two women laughed. "I don't know about you, but I'm ready to drop." Holly went straight to her husband and wound her arms around his waist. "After the day we've had, I vote for a good night's sleep for everybody. We'll tackle everything fresh in the morning."

"Troy talked with his grandmother," Jillian added, getting Michael and Edward up to speed on what had been going on outside of this protection brainstorming session. "His aunt agreed to let Dexter stay with her family indefinitely, and the hospital is keeping LaKeytah until arrangements for home health care assistance can be arranged. And guess who's going to be doing physical therapy with her on her wrist and hand? As long as it doesn't interfere with her insurance coverage, I figured doing some pro bono work was the best way I could make up for the attack."

Michael bit back the urge to point out that *she* wasn't responsible for any attack. Loverboy's skewed logic and growing penchant for violence were the only cause to blame. But Jillian couldn't be swayed from accepting some of the guilt.

"Then we got Troy and Mike to bed after teaching them Hearts and letting them beat us."

"Hey, I wasn't letting anyone win," Holly protested with a smile. "Those boys are sharp. You put them together as a team and they're unstoppable."

Michael appreciated the compliment about his son, even managed to generate a smile as he turned back to the group. "That's a testament to all the progress Jillian's made with them. Before Mike started physical therapy with her, I could barely get him to come out of his room. Now she's got him kicking ass and taking names."

"That's the Jillian brand of magic," Holly concurred. "She's always had a way of bringing out the best in people."

No one said the words, but judging by the sudden pall in the room, Michael suspected they were all thinking the same thing. Jillian's big heart had unknowingly touched Loverboy's, and brought out the absolute worst in the man.

Holly quickly went over and hugged her sister. "I'm sorry, sweetie. I've been trying to keep your mind off him all night."

"That's impossible." Jillian hugged back just as tightly. "I love you for trying, though. And for listening."

Holly pulled away and brushed a wayward strand of hair off Jillian's face. "You know, if the stress of all this gets to be too overwhelming—"

"Don't worry." Jillian pulled away and mimicked her sister's tender gesture, tucking one of Holly's dark curls behind her ear. "I'm not going to go off the deep end and start looking for a fix."

"What I was going to say, smarty-pants, is that you can call me anytime if you need to talk. Or see if Dr. Randolph is available. I know you haven't used for years and I know you're a grown woman now." Edward stepped forward, draping his arm around Holly's shoulder and backing up the message. "But that doesn't mean you have to cope with everything yourself."

"I won't."

"You don't have to take care of anybody but you right now."

"Yes, ma'am."

Holly ignored the teasing sarcasm and turned to Michael. "I asked her if she wanted to come home with us. She said she wants to stay here."

"That's fine with me." It was the only way Michael wanted it right now.

"Don't let her run off on any wild-goose chases," Holly cautioned. "She'll try."

Michael had already learned as much. "I know."

"I'll be good," Jillian promised, hugging Holly and Edward both and ushering them toward the front door of the house. "I'll let KCPD handle the investigation into Blake's murder. Now go. I need everyone well rested and on their A game tomorrow if you're going to be solving murders."

There was another round of trading hugs and shaking hands and saying good-night. Once Edward and Holly had driven away, Michael made a quick check of the house and grounds before bolting the door and turning out the lights. The boys were asleep. The house was secure. His gun had never left his side.

He found Jillian back in his office, staring out the window into the overcast night, hugging her arms around her middle. She'd changed into a pair of jeans and a long-sleeve T-shirt, hiding all of her injuries except for the stitches and bruise on her chin beneath her clothes and long hair. But he knew they were there. She stood tall and strong, but he knew how fragile she was inside. And when she turned to face him, he didn't buy the brittle smile on her lips.

"So did you and Edward decide my fate?"

He wasn't going to answer that loaded question. Instead, he held out his hand and hoped that Jillian would take it. "Holly was right. It's been a long, exhausting day. We both need our rest."

Though she took his hand and let him lead her upstairs to his bedroom, weary or not, Jillian made it clear she hadn't changed her resolve about finding Loverboy. "I promised to let you guys work on Blake's murder. But if there's anything I can do to make that rat come out of the woodwork, I'm going to. Of course, I'm hoping you or Edward or Eli will be there to catch him when he does."

Michael peeled off his torn sweater and tossed it into the trash can. "And how are you going to do that? Go through that list of yours and ask every man who has ever called you Jilly whether or not he tried to kill you today?"

"If I have to."

He carefully laid his gun and badge on the lamp table beside the bed, replaying in his head each of the threats from that tape. He'd heard that kind of sick rhetoric before and had seen first-

hand where that kind of obsession could lead—
and how little he could really do to stop it.

"Jillian." He circled around the foot of the
bed and stopped her in the middle of changing
into the T-shirt she slept in, taking her by the
shoulders and giving her a slight shake. "I can't
live through you becoming another Daphne
Mullins. What if I'm not there when this guy
shows up again? What if I can't save you?"

"Do you want to live with that kind of fear
and doubt the rest of your life?" Green eyes,
devoid of the hope and humor he'd once seen
there, looked into his. "I don't think I can."

With that, Michael released her. He let her
have the bathroom first and then quickly
brushed his teeth, turned off the lights and
slipped under the covers. She lay on the far
side of the bed, curled into a ball, facing away
from him. Not exactly an invitation to cuddle
or try to make his point one last time.

Maybe he'd been foolish to ever consider a
future with Jillian Masterson. Not because of
the age difference that had once worried him.
Not because he wanted her focus to be on
Mike's continuing recovery. Not because she
was headstrong and compassionate and driven
to get involved helping others, even when it
meant putting herself at risk.

He'd be a fool to plan a future with Jillian. Because he'd loved and lost before. And he wasn't sure he was strong enough to love and lose again.

Still, when the nightmare snuck into her dreams again, Michael was there to wake her and hold her and wipe away her tears. When she asked him to remind her what it was like to be cared for by a man she could trust, Michael stripped them both naked and made love to her in the most tender, beautiful way he knew how. And afterward, when she fell asleep in his arms, skin to skin, his fingers in her hair, her hand over his heart, Michael knew it was too late to save himself from the heartache of loving Jillian.

He loved her. Period.

He'd never been in control of falling for her at all.

Chapter Eleven

"Eli, you look awful." Jillian planted herself in her big brother's path to stop him from wearing a rut in the carpet outside Wayne Randolph's office at Truman Medical Center. Though little could diminish his tall, lanky, chiseled good looks, the fatigue that deepened the taut lines beside his eyes and mouth was marked enough to raise the concern of any sister worth her salt.

"Thanks, champ. You're a ray of sunshine yourself."

She reached up to straighten the knot of his tie and smooth his rumpled lapel. "Sit down and relax before you fall over. I know you were up all night finishing up your case so you could get here this morning."

"Champ, if I stop moving and fall asleep, I won't be any good to you. Your friend Michael had to report to work today. Edward is following up on a lead on that green car. So it's my turn for baby-sister sitting." He leaned over to kiss the top of her head. But she read equal parts chastisement and love in his dark eyes as he straightened. "You should have told me on day one when you started having trouble with this bastard."

"There wasn't anything I couldn't handle at first." His baby-sister remark told her she'd been right to believe that he'd yet to outgrow his overprotective genes with her. "And I wasn't about to give you a reason to shortchange your work at the D.A.'s office or lose sleep over me."

Eli arched a dark eyebrow. "For your information, I completed the job that D.A. Powers sent me to do in Illinois. And the only reason I ever lose sleep over you is that, unfortunately, I taught you everything you know about being hardheaded." His gaze slipped past her to the table behind the receptionist's counter. "Hey, is that coffee?"

She grinned as her brother chased down his favorite drink, though the guilt she felt at causing him worry and taking him away from a reunion with his wife, Shauna, didn't diminish. That guilt was one of the reasons she was here this morning. The other reason? It was the first of several long shots she intended to disprove.

"Jilly?" She turned as Wayne Randolph

strolled into the reception area, his short hair slicked down by the spring rain falling outside. He set down his briefcase and opened his arms to greet her with a hug. No bad vibe there. Dr. Randolph felt too much like family for her to resist, and she walked into his arms and hugged him back. "To what do I owe the pleasure?" he asked, pulling away.

"Well, your receptionist said you didn't have any appointments until nine, and that if I got here early, maybe you could spare me a few minutes before your first patient? I hope that's okay."

"Heavens, yes." He picked up his briefcase and ushered her over to his office. "You don't need an appointment to come talk to me. Eli. Good to see you again."

He stopped when her brother approached and extended his hand. "Dr. Randolph."

The psychologist shifted his position so that his hand rested lightly at the back of Jillian's waist as he faced the not-so-subtle head-to-toe inspection from big brother. "Will you be joining us? Is this a social visit?"

"No."

Jillian touched her brother's wrist and silently urged him to lighten up a tad. She had a feeling every man was suspect in his book until proven otherwise, and she fully intended to prove that the man who'd turned her life around in rehab was no suspect. Even if, after eleven years, he still called her Jilly. "I have a couple of things I wanted to get some advice on, Doc, if you don't mind listening. And a favor to ask."

Dr. Randolph nodded. "Sometimes you just need to talk things through with an objective listener. Eli, make yourself at home. Jilly, come on inside."

Jillian settled into a familiar tweed chair while Dr. Randolph shrugged into the white lab coat he wore over his shirt and tie. He paused for a moment to clean his glasses before crossing to the desk. He tucked his briefcase underneath beside his feet and leaned forward, propping his elbows on the blotter and stee-pling his fingers together. "So what's troubling you? Something with your brother? I remember having lots of conversations about him being strict and overbearing."

"That was my teenage perspective. He was pretty young himself when Mom and Dad died and he took on the task of raising Holly and me. We've worked through all that." For a moment, Jillian felt like kicking off her shoes and curling her legs beneath her in the chair the way she'd sat so many times in Dr. Randolph's company in the past. But she was older now, stronger, too, she hoped. And since he was giving up his time for her, she'd skip the reminiscing and get down to business. "No, I'm having a little trouble with a different relationship."

"What kind of relationship?" Even though this was an informal session, he pulled a mechanical pencil from his pocket and began jotting notes.

"The girl-boy kind."

He raised a bushy eyebrow. "You want dating advice? Not exactly my area of expertise."

"Maybe not. But you always did have a way of helping me think more clearly. After these past few weeks, I find myself second-guessing everything I do or say."

He sat back in his chair, tapping his pencil against his chin. "Because of this boy?"

"Man, Doc," she corrected. "This guy is definitely a man." She smiled at the vivid image of Michael Cutler's tall, whipcord body and piercing blue eyes. True, there might be some silver sprinkled in with the coal-black hair on his head and chest, but that only added some interest to the mix. His age didn't make him a mature man. It was more about his patience and caring and determination. His confidence. His skills as a protector—and a lover. No, there was nothing boyish at all about Michael Cutler. "With everything I've been through, I don't think I could be interested in anyone who had too much little boy in him."

"I've never known you to have a relationship before." Dr. Randolph adjusted his glasses to gauge her reactions to his words. "I know you've dated—I'd be surprised if a beautiful young woman like you didn't. But I always thought your trust issues kept you from committing to a relationship."

"Oh, I trust him." Michael was the first person she'd told about Loverboy—okay, so he'd discovered that letter and forced her to tell. But they'd shared so much this past week—heated arguments, quiet conversations. Fear. Laughter. She'd given him her body. She'd given him her heart. None of that could have happened without trusting Michael.

"I meant trusting yourself to make the right choices." Dr. Randolph was leaning forward again, probing for deeper answers. "You used to talk about the bad choices you made when you were young. I don't think you'd be talking to me if you believed you'd chosen the right man."

Jillian scooted to the edge of her chair. Perhaps she hadn't explained the problem clearly enough. "My feelings aren't the problem, Doc. Convincing him that we belong together—that we could really make it work—that's where I'm running into problems."

"Why is that?"

"Because he's older than me. We share a physical attraction. But sometimes I think…"

"What?"

Here came the second-guessing. "He thinks that I'm too young to know my own heart. Or that it'll change if someone else comes along." She gripped the arms of the chair, transferring her frustration into the nubby tweed upholstery. "It won't. He's the finest man I know. He's been there for me when I needed him the most. I've never felt this way about another man."

"Are you in love with him?"

Something fragile, yet hopeful, unfurled inside her. "Yeah. I love him. It even feels right to say it out loud. But how do I convince him?"

Dr. Randolph took the time to jot something more on his notepad. But when he looked up, he offered Jillian a paternal smile. "Be patient. He'll figure it out. Sometimes, when a man is older and set in his ways, it can be hard to believe that love has finally found him."

"Found him again," Jillian clarified. "He's a widower."

"Oh?"

Jillian was feeling better. The doc was right. Look at the patience it had taken to coax Mike, Jr., out of his wary shell. If she hadn't been so hung up with her paranoia about Loverboy's intentions, she might have been able to see that caution was a Cutler family trait. "Do you think I should say something to his son? I don't want Mike to think he's any less important to me just because I'm in love with his dad."

Dr. Randolph's pencil ripped through the top page of his pad. "Damn." He tore out the page and wadded it into a ball. When he tossed it toward the trash can and it deflected off the rim and rolled across the carpet, Jillian jumped to her feet to retrieve it for him. But Wayne Randolph was already out of his chair. He picked up the trash and dropped it into the pocket of his lab coat before Jillian could reach it. "He has a son?"

Jillian straightened when he did, sensing an irritation about him that wasn't there before. She was probably eating up too much of his time. "If it doesn't work out with his dad and me, I want Mike to understand that my feelings for him won't change."

He pulled back his sleeve and glanced at his watch.

"That's the right thing to do, isn't it?"

"Sounds to me like it's something you should discuss with this old man of yours."

"Old*er*," she corrected. "Trust me, there's nothing *old* about this guy."

"Hey, um…" Dr. Randolph pulled down his sleeve and turned to Jillian with an apologetic smile. "Sorry to cut this short, but I really do have to prep for my nine o'clock. You said you needed a favor?"

"I'm the one who should apologize for using up your time." She went with him when he headed for the door. "Do you remember anyone else from my rehab days who called me Jilly instead of Jillian? I know Isaac Rush did—still does."

The doc halted abruptly and caught Jillian by the hand, demanding she look up to see the concern etched on his features. "You're not having anything to do with that street thug again, are you? I thought you were smart enough to stay away from him."

"It wasn't intentional. But I ran into him when I was helping one of my patients. Needless to say, it wasn't a happy reunion." Jillian extracted her fingers from his grip and stuck her hands into the pockets of her running jacket. There was no easy way to confess this when he was probably already thinking the worst by her mention of Isaac Rush. "I've been getting some crank calls and letters addressed to 'Jilly.'"

"And you think Rush is behind it?"

"I don't know. I'm just trying to find out every possibility."

"'Jilly,' hmm? You know I won't be able to give you patient names."

"I know. But maybe someone who works there? Or used to? Anything you can remember would be helpful."

"I'll think on it." His concern eased back into a familiar smile and he drew Jillian in for a hug. "Be careful, Jilly."

"*You* be careful, Doc," she replied, pulling away and opening the door. "I can't tell you how dangerous this guy is. I don't want to see anyone else I care about get hurt."

HE DIDN'T KNOW IF HE WANTED to love her or punish her for betraying him.

His eyes burned as he lifted his head from his work and stared at all the images watching over him. He reached up and touched the worn spot on the photograph of Jillian running laps around the hospital complex. The early morning sun shimmered in the dark mane of hair that flew out behind her. So beautiful.

He curled his gloved fingers into a fist and drew them back to his lips, breathing deeply to ease the acrid bile of frustration and disappointment that churned in his stomach. An image might be beautiful to look at. But it couldn't compare to the warmth and softness he'd felt touching her real hair.

All of these captured faces couldn't match the real thing smiling back at him. And he'd made her smile often. That had always been his gift to her—to offer her a glimpse of hope when she needed it, to make her laugh. He'd done so many things for her—made her smile, helped her with work, eased her stress, kept her safe. He'd killed for Jillian Masterson. He was ready to kill again.

And that was how she repaid him?

He swept his fist through the air, pure rage clearing a path off his desk. Papers flew. Glass shattered. Tools bounced across the floor.

That image was burned into his head more clearly than any of the others he'd collected. His sweet, innocent Jilly touching another man's face. Pulling another man close for a kiss. Sticking her tongue down another man's throat.

Smiling and kissing and holding tight to another man.

She'd probably done other things to him, too. He'd seen where she'd spent the last two nights.

He'd loved her first. He'd loved her even when Jilly hadn't loved herself. He'd given her every opportunity to see that. His love was pure and everlasting, and she was destroying it with her foolish actions.

Her adolescent lust for that other man would pass. He would forgive her the transgression. His loyalty to her would always be true.

He deserved her love.

He deserved her.

No one else could have her.

She just needed his help one more time to understand that.

His resolve firmly in place, his outrage firmly in check, he picked through the debris on his desk and lifted the sealed envelope. He brushed off the bits of glass and slipped it inside the pocket of his coat. He slipped the freshly packed magazine of bullets into his gun and tucked it into its holster.

Then he stood and fastened the front of his coat over the bulk of the special gift he wore around his chest. His stint in the army had taught him several things. How to handle a gun. How to be silent and listen. How to do the tough job when necessity called for it.

And how to protect what was rightfully his.

"HE SHOOTS. HE SCORES!" Jillian cheered as Troy's shot swished through the net. She rebounded the ball and dribbled down the free throw lane out beyond the three-point line as he spun his chair and gave chase.

A little two-on-one ball at the end of the day seemed to be the ticket for lightening everyone's mood as they waited for Michael to come pick them up at the end of Troy and Mike's PT session. Not that Mike and Troy had given her much to complain about. During a set of arm curls in the weight room, Mike had even opened up a bit about his late friend Steve. He'd been the one into lifting weights and bulking up for the football team. While both boys had enjoyed working out and working hard during football camps, Steve had been the health nut. Because of that, Steve hadn't been drinking the night of the accident that had claimed his life. He'd volunteered to be the designated driver at the underage party where Mike had tried his first beers.

It had been an offhand comment between

one weight machine and the next. But the confession gave Jillian a bit more insight into Mike's emotional state during his recovery. He wasn't just crushed over losing a friend and his ability to play football. He was probably feeling guilty about having survived the crash at all while his more responsible friend had died.

It was a discovery she'd mention to Michael. If he ever got there. Jillian's watch read 5:15. She prayed that Michael's unusual tardiness was the result of something as benign as rush-hour traffic, and not because his team had been called out to another dangerous situation. She wondered if Mike ever watched the clock that closely or worried this much about his father's late arrival.

Not at the moment, judging by the way he pushed his chair back and forth, trying to keep her away from the basket.

"Oh, no, buddy," she taunted, squaring off to shoot. "If you want to block my three-pointer, you're going to have to be taller than that."

"Masterson."

Jillian pulled up short midjump and turned to the gym's open doorway. Dylan stood there, his jacket zipped, his expression annoyed. She propped the basketball on her hip and jogged over to him. "Yeah, Smith?"

"Everyone's gone home. Are you okay to lock up or do you want me to stay until your cop friend shows up?"

"I'm good." She nodded over her shoulder, indicating the two teenagers behind her. "I won't be alone. Are you heading over to the Shamrock?"

"Not tonight." He patted his stomach, reminding her of the consequences of his last visit to the bar. "What do you want me to tell the cop sitting out front?"

"You noticed him, huh?"

"Kind of hard to miss the armed guards that have been hanging around the clinic the past few days. It makes some of my patients nervous. Hell, it makes me nervous." He pointed to his own face to indicate the bandage on her chin. "Are you sure you're ready to be back at work?"

"I'm fine." She summoned a smile. "I hope they haven't cramped your style too much." The tightness around his mouth never left his expression. "Dylan, is something wrong?"

"Nah." He shoved his hands into the pockets of his khakis and shrugged. "I guess I've got to stop hitting on you now. You and that cop are the real thing, hmm?"

"I hope so," she answered honestly. She had to shrug, too. "I know you tried. And I'm flat-tered. But, um, it just never clicked with me. And besides, there's the whole romance between coworkers thing that can get—"

"Pretty awkward. Yeah, I know."

Jillian extended her hand and an apology. "I hope we can still be friends."

After a momentary hesitation, Dylan took her hand and held on a little longer than what felt comfortable. "I'll get over it." When he finally let go, Jillian quickly returned her hands to the ball and retreated a half step. "I'll tell the officer outside you're still in here with the boys and lock the front door on my way out. The hospital corridor entrance and patio exit off the lounge are already locked. You should be safe. Good night, Jilly."

"Good…night."

Jilly? Everything inside her tensed and she hugged the ball to her stomach. No. Not Dylan. She couldn't have worked side by side with the man for this long and not have known, not have suspected.

She didn't take another full breath until he was out the door. She pressed the back of her hand to each cheek, feeling feverish and unsettled. *Idiot.*

A lot of people called her Jilly. Didn't make them all stalkers and killers. Dylan's mood could be chalked up to spicy peppers and a bruised ego. If he had wanted to hurt her, he'd have had more opportunity than most, given all the hours they worked together. His was one more name she could scratch off her list.

"Hey, Jillian," Troy called. "Are we playin' or what?"

Concentrate on the task at hand and let Edward run his investigation to track down Loverboy. Michael would be here soon enough and then her world would right itself again.

She pulled her ponytail away from the perspiration at the back of her neck and spun around to face her opponents. "Definitely playing."

She ran the ball past Troy, then dribbled a circle around Mike's chair. When she turned to the basket to shoot, she had a wall of Mike Cutler, Jr., in her face.

He was on his feet, his leg braces locked, his hand in the air, positioned to block her shot. Jillian rocked back on her heels, beaming with a double dose of pride and awe. "Wow. Look at you. Standing on your own. Balancing yourself."

Despite the obvious clench of his jaw as he struggled to maintain his upright posture, Mike wore a bit of a devilish grin himself. "You said I needed to be taller."

"I thought basketball was lame." She quoted him from an earlier session.

"It is." He pulled the ball from her hands and sat back in his chair with a wicked grin. "But losing's worse."

With a round of cheers from Troy, he wheeled to the basket and banked a shot off the backboard. Jillian couldn't help it. She absolutely couldn't help herself. As soon as Mike and Troy were done butting fists and trading celebratory gibes, she reached around Mike's shoulders and hugged him. "I am so proud of you, big guy."

He patted her arm where it crossed his chest and tilted his ear against hers in a cool teenage guy version of a hug. "Thanks."

Pulling away before she embarrassed Mike, Jillian traded high fives with both boys. "Great workout today, guys. I think this rates a call to your dad to tell him the good news."

Mike's cheeks were pink. "All I did was stand up."

She leaned over and pressed a kiss to one of those pink cheeks and watched it redden. "Mike, what you did today is as big as the first day I left rehab and faced the world on my own.

"My phone's in my office. I'm calling your dad." She pulled her keys from the pocket of her slacks. She'd truly feel like celebrating if she

knew Michael was on his way. Maybe surrounded by father and son and friend, she could
actually push aside her fears about Loverboy
for a little while. "Hey, guys?" As long as they
were feeling good, she'd keep Mike and Troy
moving. Hurrying over to the corner of the gym,
she unlocked the storage closet and rolled out
the ball bin. "Will you two gather up the basket-
balls and put them in the storage closet for me?"

"Will do."

"Thanks, guys."

With a buoyancy to her stride that belied her
beat-up knees, Jillian headed out of the gym
and down the corridor to her office. She tried
to focus on the joy she felt at Mike's small
victory instead of noticing the stillness of the
clinic without patients and staff to create the
normal buzz of noise that filled the rooms. She
tried to imagine how thrilled Michael would be
when she told him that Mike had made signifi-
cant progress in his attitude toward rehabilitation today instead of imagining the curious eyes
watching her from darkened offices and
shadowed corners.

But when she rounded the corner to her
office, Jillian quickly pulled back and flattened
herself against the wall. She pressed her fingers

against her lips to stifle the urge to call out or gasp with surprise.

Ever so slowly, she held her breath and peeked around the corner again. *Oh, no. Please no.*

She pulled back against the wall again and clutched at the wallpaper behind her, willing her knees not to buckle.

There was a man at her door with a ring of keys, jerking on the knob and cursing beneath his breath. "Changed the damn lock here, too. Ah, Jilly, Jilly. What am I going to do with you?"

It could be coincidence—it could be lousy timing that he was here at this moment trying to break in. But Jillian knew. After all this time. After all the letters, the professions of love—after fear and murder had changed her life—she knew.

It was him. He was here.

With feet and heart like lead, she crept back along the corridor, barely daring to breathe as the man she'd known for so many years damned her and praised her with every other sentence.

Jillian's first intention was to get outside to the cop assigned to watch her until Michael showed up to relieve him. But he'd hear the door opening. A phone call from the front desk would make even more noise.

And then she remembered the boys.

She remembered LaKeytah Anthony's battered body and Blake Rivers's frozen dead face.

Training her ear to any sign that Loverboy was following her, she dashed into the gym. Her expression alone must have told the boys that something was wrong.

Mike pulled the ball he'd been about to shoot into the storage bin back into his lap. "What is it?"

Jillian grabbed Troy's chair and pushed him inside the closet. "Not a word. Either of you," she warned.

"What's wrong?" Troy asked.

"Shh."

Mike was already following them in. She plucked the basketball from his grasp and turned him so that both wheelchairs would fit. "If either of you has your cell phone, set it to silent and text 9-1-1."

Troy pulled out his phone.

"Jillian?" Mike caught her wrist as she climbed over his legs.

She had every intention of pulling the door shut and hiding in the closet with them. But then she heard the footsteps and knew she couldn't risk discovery and anyone else being hurt. She twisted free and squeezed his hand. "Text your father. Tell him Loverboy is here. He'll know what to do. And please, not one sound."

Without another backward look, she shut the door behind her. At the first tiny clank of chair wheels tangling with each other, Jillian started dribbling the ball. She made as much noise as she could, charging the basket and making a perfect layup, drawing attention away from the closet.

She never got the chance to make a second shot.

"Hello, Jilly. I suppose this meeting was inevitable. I'm glad I can finally tell you the truth."

Jillian turned around and looked straight into the barrel of Wayne Randolph's gun.

Chapter Twelve

"I need eyes on this guy. Somebody tell me they've got a way into the gym."

Michael Cutler had been a cop for too many years to see this day. An emergency text message from his own son at the same time he got a 9-1-1 call from Dispatch? Both telling him Mike and Troy were trapped inside the medical center's physical therapy clinic with a guy who claimed to have a bomb, and that said bastard was holding the woman he loved at gunpoint.

Edward Kincaid had finally gotten the break they needed, following up on fifty-one green cars in the Kansas City area until he tracked down the only owner with a connection to Jillian.

Dr. Wayne Randolph.

Mild-mannered miracle worker from the Boatman Rehabilitation Clinic. Jillian's mentor. Father figure.

Loverboy.

Eli Masterson had gone through Randolph's
office with a fine-tooth comb and found a
wadded-up ball of torn paper with the word
Jilly scribbled on it over and over. With
Kincaid obtaining a search warrant, Michael's
own team had been in the process of conducting a raid on Randolph's home when Mike's
text message had come.

Dad
Trub at PTC
J taken
Gun/Bomb/Help

In Randolph's basement office, they'd found
.45-caliber bullets, materials to make a pipe
bomb, a set of copied keys and the sickest
display of obsession Michael had ever seen.
Pictures of Jillian tacked to a bulletin board. A
newspaper photo from her high school basketball championship game. A handwritten thank-
you card that credited Randolph with saving
her life in rehab. Candid shots of Jillian—from
the clinic, at her apartment building, hurrying
down 10th Street near Troy's apartment
building in No-Man's Land.

Maybe Randolph had sensed they were

closing in. Maybe something Jillian had shared in their session this morning had set him off. Whatever his motives, whatever his reasoning, Randolph had Jillian locked inside a window-less half-court gymnasium, carrying a pistol and a bomb.

Night was here. Rain was falling.

Mike and Troy were missing, presumably also in harm's way.

It was the worst-case scenario of Michael's life.

And SWAT Team 1 had gotten the call.

He rubbed at his chest through the Kevlar vest he wore. The protective armor was supposed to protect the vital organs inside his body. Yet he was already suffering from the emotional bullet that had pierced his heart.

It was impossible to shut down the fear and anger he felt. He'd promised to keep Jillian safe. And now he might lose her before he ever had the chance to make things right between them.

The emotional barrage might have incapaci-tated a different man. But Michael Cutler had twenty-two years of experience and the best training KCPD could provide running through his veins. He spoke into the radio at the command center they'd set up in the clinic parking lot and asked for a situation report. "I need a sit rep now."

One by one, his men reported in.

Holden Kincaid was on the roof. "Negative, sir."

Trip Jones had secured the clinic's main entrance. "Negative."

Alex Taylor was on his belly outside the gym's locked doors. "I've got two thermal signatures in the center of the gym, but I'm blind here."

Michael waited a few seconds more for his sergeant to report in. "Delgado?"

"I'm checking out some mice in the wall."

"Come again?"

Rafe Delgado's voice dropped to a whisper. "I'm coming in through the patio entrance. I heard something I want to check out. But no visual yet, sir."

"Keep me posted."

Tossing the handheld radio back into the gear box at the back of the SWAT van, Michael turned to Edward Kincaid. "At least tell me we've got the rest of the clinic evacuated and a perimeter set up."

Edward nodded. "Your men's room-to-room check hasn't turned up anything. The hospital staff and patients in the connecting corridor area have been moved to the far end of the complex. Uniformed officers have the immediate blast area cordoned off and Bomb Squad is ready to go in on your order."

Everything about their response thus far had gone by the book. "So why don't I feel any better about this?"

"Because Jillian's the one trapped inside." Edward pulled back the front of his jacket and propped his hands at his waist. "I won't feel good about any of this until I see her out here in one piece."

Michael fingered the phone that usually served him so well. But a call to Wayne Randolph's phone had ended up at an answering service that said he wasn't responding, and a call to Jillian's phone went straight to voice mail. He couldn't negotiate with a hostage taker if he couldn't reach him.

And standing here, supervising reports that told him nothing, wasn't getting him any closer to having Jillian safely in his arms again. He needed inside that gymnasium. He needed to look Wayne Randolph in the eye and tell that murdering SOB exactly what he could do with his style of loving.

The radio crackled to life as Rafe Delgado buzzed in. Michael's senses all leaped to attention. "Captain? You're going to want to see this."

"MIKE?"

Rafe Delgado stood by the counter in the clinic lounge with his rifle on his hip and his eyes peeled as Michael swallowed his son up in a hug.

"Dad."

"Thank God you're safe." It almost didn't register that Mike was standing on his feet, hugging him back. He pulled back long enough to drop a spare Kevlar over Mike's head and closed the straps on either side of his torso. Then he palmed the side of his son's flushed face, trying to distinguish panic from excitement in his expression. "Where's your chair?"

"I had to leave it behind. Once I got the braces locked, I could move okay. It's the getting up and down that's tough."

Michael nodded. He'd want details later. For now, it was enough to know he was okay. "Rafe, let's get him out of here."

"No." Mike snatched at his arm, his balance wavering a bit at the sudden movement. "Troy's in there. So is Jillian and some creep with a gun."

"I know, son." Michael stiffened his arm to give Mike something sturdier to hold on to as he took a small step toward the patio exit where he'd come in. "As soon as my men can find a way into that gym, we're getting her out. We'll get them both out."

Mike pulled away and tottered back toward the storage closet where Rafe had discovered him. He shook off Michael's efforts to steer him back toward the patio. "I know a way in."

"How?"

Michael followed him into the closet and watched Mike push open a small door in the back. "The same way I got out."

"YOU LIED TO ME. All these years you've been lying to me."

The duct tape that bound Jillian's wrists together pricked at her skin and bruised her with every twist and pull as she tried to free herself. The desperate movements stopped abruptly when Dr. Randolph turned and walked toward her again. As far as he knew, she was sitting in the middle of the gym floor beside the leather briefcase with the pipe bomb inside, listening in rapt attention to his wandering diatribe about love and loyalty and loss.

She hoped.

He scratched his temple with the tip of his black steel pistol, dislodging his glasses and forcing him to stop and set them back into place before continuing.

Dr. Randolph had proudly shown her the bomb. Like a professor leading a classroom lecture, he'd patiently described in detail how he'd created it, how he'd learned to be a fairly decent shot in the army and how he wouldn't hesitate to use either skill if she didn't do exactly as he said.

"I taught you in rehab that you should never lie to me. I thought you'd learned your lesson." He pulled the gun from his temple and glanced at it as though surprised to discover he'd pointed it at his own head. But he didn't seem to have any qualm about pointing the gun directly at hers. Jillian jumped inside her skin, but she had no place to run, no way to fight him as long as her hands were bound like this.

All she had were her words. "I never lied to you, Doc. Maybe those first few weeks in the clinic when you asked me about how long I'd been doing drugs or what was the craziest thing I'd done to get my hands on some coke. But once I was healthy, once you helped me heal, I never told you another lie."

He shook the gun at her. "You loved me."

"I never said that."

The same mouth that had recited a sonnet to her a few minutes ago now spat nothing but contempt. "You loved me!"

When he knelt down beside her, Jillian scooted away. But he caught her by the elbow and jerked her back, peeling off a layer of skin at her wrists. She bit her lip to hide her yelp of pain. But the same lip trembled with fear when he pressed the gun to her forehead and used it to brush her bangs out of her eyes.

"You sent me cards, pictures, letters over the years. Sharing your life with me. Thanking me."

She couldn't look into his eyes. She could only follow the gun as he continued to caress her with it. "I was grateful. Your patience and caring turned my life around. I always thought of you as a friend. Maybe the closest thing I had to a father since losing my dad. I'm sure you had other patients who felt the same—"

"A father figure?" He pushed to his feet and paced away again. Jillian instantly raised her wrists to her teeth and tried to cut through the tape that way. "No. It was love. I saw the way you smiled at me each time we met."

A scuffling noise from the storage closet diverted her attention from the tape. *No!* She'd warned the boys to stay quiet. If Randolph knew they had an audience now…

"I *do* love you." She said the first thing that came to mind, praying she was loud enough to mask any noises the boys made. It might have been true, up until a couple of hours ago when she'd seen him trying to break into her office. "Just not in that way. I loved you…" She swallowed hard so she could speak the lie. "I love you like a friend, Doc. Maybe even like family. But the flowers and the love letters… I never loved you in that way."

"Lies, Jilly!" The gun swung her way again as he stalked toward her. "All lies!"

He knelt beside her again, but this time to pull the pipe bomb from inside his briefcase and lay it across her lap. Every muscle constricted, trying to draw her body away from the lethal pipe. But there was no escape. The heaviness and instability of the weapon weighed her down, rendered her immobile, trapped her in place next to the man who was running his fingers through the length of her ponytail and pressing kisses to strand after strand as he spoke.

"I was content to love you from a distance because I knew you weren't ready to be loved. That was always one of the hardest lessons for you to accept, Jilly, dear." He paused to inhale the scent of her hair and Jillian's stomach clenched against the urge to gag. "You've always questioned your own worth. How many conversations have we had over the years about you feeling like you didn't deserve to have good things happen to you? You were barely more than a child when you lost your parents. That's more than most adults can cope with. Yes, you made some bad choices, got involved with Rivers and Rush and other men who never had your best interests at heart. But that doesn't mean you have to pay for those mistakes the rest of your life."

Jillian sucked in a shuddering breath and he rewarded her by running his fingers through her hair again.

"So beautiful. Inside and out." He stopped playing with her hair long enough to curl the fuse connected to the bomb around his finger and then pull it straight and smooth it out against her thigh. "You should be proud of everything you've accomplished, Jilly. I am. You deserve to be happy. You deserve to be loved. I was only waiting for you to be ready to accept me. I waited until you were old enough, until you were confident enough. Then I began to woo you. And how do you repay me?"

He waited until she tilted her tear-filled eyes up to him to answer.

"You gave your love to another man."

Michael. Yes, she loved him. In his skewed view of reality, Wayne Randolph was exactly right. For years, Jillian always believed she had a debt to pay society before she could love and be loved. He'd helped her finally learn that lesson.

She loved Michael Cutler. And if she ever, ever got out of this gym alive, she would do whatever was necessary to earn his love in return.

"I taught you how to love," Wayne continued. "I thought our ages would be the thing to keep us apart. And then I see you kissing another older man. *We're* supposed to be together. You're supposed to love *me.*"

"What are you going to do, Doc?" Jillian asked. "Are you going to kill me for disappointing you?"

"For betraying me, you mean?"

Why had she ever thought the eyes behind those glasses had been kind? "I don't love you, Wayne."

"What?"

"I don't love you."

The shock of her quietly rebellious words must have distracted Wayne from the sound of a door opening and closing softly behind her.

"Randolph."

The doctor jumped to his feet, his gun swinging toward that beloved, deep voice at the back of the gym. "You! Get out of here!"

"Easy, Randolph." Jillian turned her head just enough to see Michael holding up his left hand in surrender as he slowly pulled his gun from his thigh holster and set it on the floor. "I'm just here to talk. I'm Michael Cutler, KCPD. My men and I needed to see what the situation was like in here. See if there was anything we could do to help. Jillian, you all right?"

She didn't know whether to weep with relief or yell at him to run and get as far away from her as he could. "I have a bomb in my lap."

"It'll be all right, sweetheart. Bomb Squad's outside, waiting for my signal."

"Sweetheart?" Dr. Randolph took a step toward the unarmed cop. "So you're the one. You couldn't keep your hands off her, could you? You couldn't keep your hands off my Jilly."

Michael kept his hands in the air, a gesture meant to show he posed no threat, though the uniform and SWAT vest and focused eyes said something different. "I'm a negotiator, Randolph. Like I said, I'm just here to talk. Now I can reassure my men that everything is under control in here."

"Liar." Wayne advanced another step. "I'm

surrounded by liars. You're here to get your tramp back." And another. "You can't have her!"

"Why don't you put the gun down and we'll discuss this?"

"There's nothing to discuss. Jilly is mine. She loves *me*. We will be together one way or another."

"Put the gun down, Randolph."

He was too close to Michael. Even a lousy shot couldn't miss at that range. "Michael. Please just leave. I don't want anyone else to get hurt. Please."

"I'm not leaving you."

"Get. Out." Wayne wrapped both hands around the gun and took aim.

"Put the gun down or I'll take it from you."

"Michael!"

"Get out!" Wayne pulled the trigger and Jillian screamed.

"No!"

Michael jerked back against the gym wall and sank to the floor.

"No!" She tried to turn, tried to steady the bomb on her thighs and get to him to help. "Michael!"

Randolph came back and grabbed her ponytail, spinning her around to face him. A million pinpricks of pain stabbed across her scalp, and burned her eyes with tears. "I hate you, Wayne! I hate you!"

He ignored her kicks, ignored her screams, ignored her pain. He pulled a lighter from his pocket and reached for the fuse. "It's you and me, Jilly. Forever."

"Randolph! Get away from her!"

"What?"

"Michael?"

Wayne picked up his gun, took aim as Jillian whirled around.

"Drop it!"

Michael already had a bead on Wayne when the doctor fired.

Jillian jerked at each gunshot. Held her breath.

She watched the circle of blood bloom across the front of Wayne Randolph's jacket as his knees buckled and he collapsed to the floor. Dead.

"Jillian?" Michael was at her side in an instant, his boot on Randolph's gun, taking no chances as he slid it from his lifeless grasp and tucked it into the back of his uniform. "Sweetheart, you're not hit, are you?" Then he was on his knees beside her, carefully lifting the pipe bomb and placing it back inside the briefcase. "Jillian, are you hurt?"

His hands were on her face now, running

along her arms and down her legs. The shock of the last few seconds hadn't entirely worn off as she pushed aside his assessing hands and caught his face between her own bound hands. He stilled long enough for her to see the clear, focused strength shining in those dark blue eyes. She shook her head in disbelief. "He shot you."

"That's what the body armor's for." Michael leaned in and covered her lips in a quick, hard, life-affirming kiss. Then he drew a wicked-looking knife from his belt and sliced through the tape at her wrists, freeing her.

He pulled those same wrists around his neck and scooped her off the floor and into his arms. "I'm not hurt. I can walk."

"Humor me, okay, sweetheart?"

Jillian tightened her arms around his neck and smiled. "Okay."

"And do me a favor. Press the button on that radio on my shoulder." She pushed the button and Michael turned his chin to his shoulder, carrying her back to the closet where she hoped the boys were still safely hidden, snapping orders all the way. "Taylor? Take down that door and get the bomb squad in here now. Trip, I need evac assistance with a wheelchair-bound hostage in the gym. Kincaid? Make sure the ambulance is ready. Delgado? Tell Mike his plan worked. We're coming out."

"I UNDERSTAND SURVIVOR'S GUILT, son."

Michael couldn't remember the last time he'd had this long or this meaningful a conversation with Mike. Certainly not since the accident and Pam's death. Sitting together on the back step of the SWAT van while Edward Kincaid supervised the debriefing of everyone in the aftermath of a hostage crisis wasn't how he'd pictured this breakthrough moment. But Michael wouldn't have changed the drippy weather or beehive of official activity for anything. His son was finally talking to him.

"You don't think I would have died in your mother's place?" he explained. "I'm the tough guy—the one with the dangerous job. She was kind, gentle, loving—smarter than I'll ever be. There's not a day that goes by that I don't think it should have been me."

Mike swiped at the tears in his eyes and nodded. "Steve was the good one. He was being responsible by not drinking. He was being a good friend by taking me home when I'd had too much. I worked hard in the classes I liked and blew off the others. But Steve…he worked hard at everything. He wanted to be a firefighter like his dad. He had something useful to give the world. I was just going to play football. It should have been me who died in that crash."

Michael wrapped his arm around his shoulders and hugged him to his side. "I'll argue with you on that one. Grief is a lousy thing to deal with. For months after your mom died, I was just going through the motions. I shut down inside. But then you got hurt, and I kind of woke up from that guilty haze I'd been living in. I realized I had a job to do—the most important one in the world."

"Being a cop?"

"Being your father." He loosened his grip, and was heartened when Mike didn't immediately slide away. "You know what else I realized? That I was dishonoring your mother. No, I couldn't save her. Nobody could. God's got her now because He probably needed somebody to get his books in order."

Mike's mouth tilted with half a grin. "Yeah, she was a freak about organizing stuff, wasn't she? Classroom parties. Little League fundraisers. The football parents' booster club."

"She was a pro, wasn't she?"

"Yeah."

Michael caught his son's last tear with his

knuckle and flicked it away. "I finally got my act together and realized mourning your mom, feeling guilty about her death—just going through the motions of living—would really tick her off. Your mom would have wanted me, wanted *us,* to really live. To make a difference in the world. To do our jobs well. Set goals—achieve them. Make friends. Feel things."

"Sounds a lot like the way Jillian lives."

"Yeah." That was an admission to make. "She's a pretty gung-ho lady, isn't she?"

"I was thinking I could do some of that, too. You know, setting goals, making a difference?" Mike locked his braces into place and pushed to his feet. Michael stood, too, intending to help him, but it was pretty clear that moving from a seat into his wheelchair wasn't a big deal anymore. Another reason to thank Jillian. "I thought about majoring in physical therapy in college, or becoming a sports trainer or coach. Troy and I even talked about how we could open some kind of training center together."

"Get through high school first." Michael did his fatherly duty and reminded Mike to keep those priorities in the right order. "I don't think I've ever been prouder of you, son, than I am of you tonight. I love you."

"Love you, too, Dad." When Michael started to lean in for another hug, Mike put up one hand and turned his chair with another. Okay. Real world. Enough mush for one night.

And that was when they discovered they weren't alone. Having answered all of Edward's preliminary questions, Jillian was standing a few feet away, hugging her arms around her middle. The sprinkle of rain still falling couldn't mask the tears running down her face.

Michael felt a tug on his sleeve and bent down to hear Mike whisper, "Now go give her the same speech. Mom would like her. *I* like her. Don't screw it up."

With a nod and a wave, Mike rolled past her and joined Troy under the awning of the PT clinic's entrance, where Trip and Delgado were regaling the boys with stories that earned them lots of high fives and laughs. A weight had lifted from his heart tonight, and Michael decided to take his son's advice.

He reached inside the back of the van and pulled out his black KCPD jacket as Jillian approached.

She smiled. "Mike's my hero tonight, finding a way to get you inside the gym so you could save me. He's a good kid."

"He's a great kid." Michael draped the jacket around her shoulders and all kinds of primitive, possessive, perfect feelings started drumming through his blood.

"I was scared I was going to lose both of you tonight."

"I love you."

He said it bluntly, startling her. As those beautiful green eyes returned to their normal size, he startled her again by fisting his hands around the collar of the jacket and pulling her up into his kiss. He took his own sweet time easing the surprise from her lips, then tracing the seam with his tongue and urging them to part so that he could slip inside and taste the essence of Jillian herself. He was pretty well kissed himself by the time he came up for air and rested his forehead against hers with a contented sigh.

"I feel young and strong when I'm with you. You gave me back my son." He covered her hands where they clung to the collar of his uniform with his own. "You make me give a damn about living again."

"I love you, Michael." The words sounded right. Felt right. Were right. "I love your son. And I'm damn lucky that you feel something for me, too."

"Not just 'something,' sweetheart. Love. I feel love."

"So what are we going to do?" She wound her arms around his neck and pulled herself closer. "Do you think we can make a relationship work?"

He slipped his hands beneath the jacket she wore and sealed the embrace. "Are you still going to go on your crusades to save kids who've been through hell?"

"After I take a bit of a break to rest up, yes. Are you still going to be a SWAT cop?"

"Yeah. I think I may have the knack for it." She smiled and the moment was complete. "I'm still going to be a father and I'm hoping I'm going to be a husband again, as well."

"A husband?"

"Yeah. To you." He was dead serious now. In that controlled, I'm-the-boss way that he normally did so well. "Mike told me not to screw this up, so I thought I'd better put it out there before you get away from me—or I lose you to some other man."

But Jillian saw right through the tough guy facade to the man who would forever be vulnerable to a tall, leggy woman with sweet green eyes and coffee-colored hair. She gently cupped his jaw. "You are never going to lose me, Michael Cutler. I love you. And it would be the greatest honor of my life to be your wife."

"And that's a firm yes?"

"Haven't you figured it out yet, Captain? I didn't slow my steps because of your age. I was just waiting for you to catch me."

"When did you ever slow down for me?"

Her lips curved into a sly grin. "Just kiss me."

* * * * *

Look for more books of heart pounding romantic suspense in Julie Miller's
THE PRECINCT *series,*
wherever Harlequin Intrigue books are sold!

*Harlequin Intrigue top author Delores Fossen
presents a brand-new series of
breathtaking romantic suspense!*
TEXAS MATERNITY: HOSTAGES
*The first installment available May 2010:
THE BABY'S GUARDIAN*

Shaw cursed and hooked his arm around Sabrina.

Despite the urgency that the deadly gunfire created, he tried to be careful with her, and he took the brunt of the fall when he pulled her to the ground. His shoulder hit hard, but he held on tight to his gun so that it wouldn't be jarred from his hand.

Shaw didn't stop there. He crawled over Sabrina, sheltering her pregnant belly with his body, and he came up ready to return fire.

This was obviously a situation he'd wanted to avoid at all cost. He didn't want his baby in the middle of a fight with these armed fugitives, but when they fired that shot, they'd left him no choice. Now, the trick was to get Sabrina safely out of there.

"Get down," someone on the SWAT team yelled from the roof of the adjacent building.

Shaw did. He dropped lower, covering Sabrina as best he could.

There was another shot, but this one came from a rifleman on the SWAT team. Shaw didn't look up, but he heard the sound of glass being blown apart.

The shots continued, all coming from his men, which meant it might be time to try to get Sabrina to better cover. Shaw glanced at the front of the building.

So that Sabrina's pregnant belly wouldn't be smashed against the ground, Shaw eased off her and moved her to a sitting position so that her back was against the brick wall. They were close. Too close. And face-to-face.

He found himself staring right into those sea-green eyes.

How will Shaw get Sabrina out?
Follow the daring rescue
and the heartbreaking
aftermath in THE BABY'S GUARDIAN
by Delores Fossen,
available May 2010
from Harlequin Intrigue.

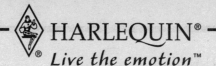

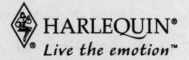

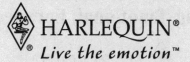

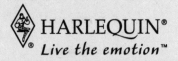

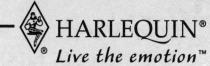

HARLEQUIN®
Live the emotion™

Love, Home & Happiness

HARLEQUIN® *Blaze™*

Red-hot reads.

 Harlequin® Historical
Historical Romantic Adventure!

HARLEQUIN® *Romance*

From the Heart, For the Heart

HARLEQUIN®
INTRIGUE
Breathtaking Romantic Suspense

Medical Romance™...
love is just a heartbeat away

HARLEQUIN®
Presents
Seduction and Passion Guaranteed!

HARLEQUIN® *Super Romance*

Exciting, Emotional, Unexpected

SUSPENSE
RIVETING INSPIRATIONAL ROMANCE

Watch for our new series of
edge-of-your-seat suspense novels.
These contemporary tales
of intrigue and romance
feature Christian characters
facing challenges to their faith...
and their lives!

**NOW AVAILABLE IN REGULAR
& LARGER-PRINT FORMATS**

Steeple
Hill®

Visit:
www.SteepleHill.com